"So, Suzy," Donna asked, "who're you fixing your womanly wiles on now?"

I looked desperately around the lunchroom. I just couldn't admit that Barry was still always on my mind—not after I'd told Donna I was over him and ready to go out with other guys.

That was when I spotted *him* in the food line. He wasn't gorgeous, but he was cute, real cute.

I nodded over toward the boy. "That's someone I'm interested in there," I said, even though I'd never noticed him before.

"Aha! Mike Kelly! I'll have to find out more about him, and then we can plot how to get him to ask you out. Oh, don't look so shocked, Suzy. I'll be subtle about it."

"But—" I stopped. How could I protest when I had just said that I was available for dates? "Don't start trying to matchmake, please," I said sternly. "Remember, I'm out to have a good time and see lots of people this year. I'm through with that just-one-boy stuff."

I was even beginning to believe it myself.

Too Much to Lose

Suzanne Rand

BANTAM BOOKS
TORONTO · NEW YORK · LONDON · SYDNEY

RL 4, IL age 11 and up

TOO MUCH TO LOSE
A Bantam Book / November 1983

Cover photo by Pat Hill

ISBN 0-553-23745-4

Published simultaneously in the United States and Canada

PRINTED IN THE UNITED STATES OF AMERICA

O   0 9 8 7 6 5 4 3 2 1

Too Much to Lose

Chapter One

I'll never forget the day Barry broke up with me. We were going to go to the lake, our usual hangout on sunny summer days like this one. I had chosen my favorite bathing suit, a blue two-piece with white polka dots, and had thrown a red tank top and white shorts on over it. Checking myself in my full-length mirror, I thought I looked pretty good. I'd lost a few pounds so my legs looked longer and slimmer; my skin was tanned golden, and the sun brought out the red highlights in my brown hair.

I ran a comb through my bangs and grabbed a pair of sunglasses. As I was on my way downstairs, my mother yelled to me, "Barry's here, honey."

"Coming," I called.

Barry was, as always, perfectly dressed. He was wearing a really stylish pair of navy cotton pants with a white sports shirt and a bandanna, the same sky blue color as his eyes. His curly blond hair had gotten even lighter in the summer sun. What a gorgeous guy. We'd been going out for six months, and I still wasn't tired of looking at him. I was always glad to be seen with him and to be known as his girlfriend.

I kissed him lightly on the cheek. "Hi, where's your towel? Aren't you going swimming today?"

"No, not today, but I'll walk with you. I wanted to talk."

"OK," I said as I slung my bag over my shoulder. " 'Bye, Mom," I called out and waved casually as we walked out the door.

Barry didn't say a word until I asked, "Well, what's up?"

He started slowly. "I've been wanting to tell you something. This is really hard to say. . . ."

"What's the matter, Barry?"

"It's just that I—well, I've met this other girl."

I stopped walking and turned to face him. "What?"

"She works at the supermarket. I should have said something sooner, but—"

"You're kidding, aren't you?" I interrupted.

"I'm not, Suzy," he said.

"How long have you been seeing her?" I asked.

"I met her a month ago."

"You mean, you were seeing us *both* at the same time?"

"I'm sorry, Suzy," he said. "I wanted to find out if it was the real thing. I mean, you're great, Suzy, really—you always will be. It's just that—"

"You don't want to go out with me anymore," I whispered.

He nodded sheepishly. "Well . . . yes." He looked away. "I know I waited a long time to tell you."

"Do I know her?" I asked, not believing we were having this conversation.

"No, she goes to Central High. I knew you'd understand, Suzy."

"Well, I don't." I marched away from him, but he grabbed my shoulder and turned me around to face him again.

"Listen, Suzy. I wanted to tell you before

3

this—honest—but I just couldn't. I had to be sure!"

"And now you're sure." I felt tears starting to burn behind my eyelids.

"Look, Suze, that's all I've got to say." Barry looked at me and saw the tears in my eyes. "I'm really sorry about everything, Suze."

"Sure." I swallowed hard.

He patted my shoulder. "See you around, OK?"

"Sure," I mumbled again and turned away quickly as he walked off.

I ran as fast as I could to the lake, gulping back tears all the way. Luckily, no one from our crowd was there yet, just a bunch of little kids on the far side. I was glad no one was around to watch me fall apart. How would I ever tell Donna, or any of my other friends?

I spread out my towel and lay down, my eyes closed. I wished I could shut out my feelings as easily as I shut out the sun.

"Hi, Suzy. Getting to work on your tan?" I heard Donna say before long. "You're really getting dark."

"Yeah, but I'd like to be a little darker." I looked up at her and tried to sound cheerful.

Donna pulled her towel out of her bag and spread it out next to mine. "Hey," she said

4

suddenly. "Your eyes are all red. What's the matter?"

I looked away, and then I blurted it out. "Barry and I . . . decided . . . not to see each other anymore." I *couldn't* tell her the truth.

"What?" Donna practically shouted. "If you *both* decided, then why have you been crying?"

She looked so concerned and upset that I just broke down. "Oh, Donna! He's been going out with someone else for the past month."

"That's terrible! How did it happen?"

"I can't talk about it now," I said. "I don't even want to think about him!"

"OK, Suzy." Donna gave my hand a squeeze and switched on her portable radio. "But, Suzy, if you need me, I'm here to talk to," she said.

"OK, thanks."

The morning dragged by with neither of us saying much to each other, which made it a lot easier for me. We left at noon, and when I got home, Mom and my sister Patty were sitting in the kitchen having lunch.

"Hi, Suzy, come join us for roast beef sandwiches," my mom offered.

I dropped my bag underneath the table and got some milk from the fridge.

One thing you've got to realize about my

sister is that she's an incredible snoop. No one can hide anything from that spying little eleven-year-old, especially not me. She just loves to pry into all my secrets. Today I knew I couldn't let Patty know anything was wrong.

"Hi, Suzy," she said. "Hey, can I go swimming with you this afternoon?"

"No, I'm not going back today," I said, trying to sound nice and cool.

"You have to if Mommy says so," she said. "Isn't that right, Mom?"

My mother took another half of a sandwich. "Suzy, it *would* be nice if you took your sister swimming today."

"I can't, Mom." I felt a lump in my throat.

"What's the matter?" Patty said suspiciously. "Had a fight with Barry or something?"

"That does it!" I said. "I'm not having any lunch, and I'm not taking you anywhere!"

I could hardly keep from crying as I ran up to my room, and once my door was safely shut behind me, I let my tears flow hard and fast. But of course Mom couldn't leave me alone to cry. When I heard her gentle knock, I hastily wiped my tears away and called through the door, "I'm busy."

"Is anything wrong, Suzy?" she asked, her voice muffled by the door.

"No, Mom. I just want to listen to some music. I'm fine."

"OK, honey," she said hesitantly. "You sure you don't have anything you want to talk about?"

"No, Mom. Thanks, anyway." I knew I couldn't tell her about Barry—not yet. It hurt too much.

For a full week after that I was in a daze. I mailed back the class ring Barry had given me during sophomore year; I couldn't stand the humiliation of handing it back in person. I moped around the house or went to the lake and sat there without talking much.

One day Donna said to me in exasperation, "Smile once in a while, Suzy. Even if you feel bad."

"I know, Donna. I'm sorry I'm such a drag. It's just that I can't seem to forget about him."

"I know you feel terrible, but if that's the kind of guy Barry's turned out to be, you're better off without him."

"I'm glad to be rid of him," I said, lying through my teeth. "I just wish I'd known sooner what he was like."

"He's gone, Suze." Her big brown eyes were

solemn. "Forget about him. It's time for you to go out and have some fun."

"You're right," I said, not bothering to explain to her that I just couldn't forget someone that easily—especially not Barry.

And that's how the summer dragged by, one miserable day after another.

Eventually I had to say something to my parents since I knew they must be wondering why Barry hadn't been coming around at all. The night I decided to tell them, I made myself sound very grown-up as I walked into the living room. It was after dinner, and my mother and father were having cake and coffee.

"Mom, Dad? I just want to talk to you about something." I tried to sound cool.

"Sure, honey," my father said. "Shoot."

"It's about Barry. We, uh, decided it was time for us both to slow down and start seeing other people."

"Sounds like a good idea to me," my father said, reaching for another slice of cake.

I was halfway there. My father was obviously happy and ready to drop the subject. But I could see that my mother was puzzled. She knew how much I liked Barry. Still, she went along with Dad.

"Well, Suzy, if that's what you want, I think it's good to give yourselves a chance." Then she said gently, "Do you and Barry plan to see each other at all?"

I wished she hadn't asked that. "I'm not sure, Mom. We'll see how it goes." I hated having to duck the subject like that, but I didn't feel I could handle any more questions.

"All we want is for you to be happy," my mother said.

I looked at the clock over the fireplace. "I'm meeting Donna at the movies. Be back around ten." I kissed them good night and left the room quickly. But as I was in the front hallway, I heard my mother talking.

"I worry about her, Jeff."

"Why? I think she's handling it very well."

"I know. But Suzy keeps her feelings locked away sometimes. Don't forget, Jeff, she really cared for Barry. And I must say, she's been very upset lately."

I tiptoed out then and closed the door quietly behind me. I didn't want to hear another word. As I walked down the tree-lined street, I was thinking, *How am I going to get through this?* Nothing could change the shriveled-up way I felt inside. And I wouldn't have admitted it to a soul, but not only was I in shock about Barry, I was also worried about having to date other boys. After six months with Barry, I just couldn't imagine what it would be like to spend a whole evening talking with a new boy. How could I ever kiss anyone else again? And after the lousy way Barry had treated me, how could I ever trust another boy again?

A month later, I saw Barry walking down the street with his arm around his brand-new girlfriend.

It was three o'clock in the afternoon, and I was bicycling home from the library. If I could have, I would have ducked down some side street and pedaled away. But since I could recognize Barry from that distance, I knew darned well he recognized me, too. Then he waved, and I knew I was trapped.

I rode up to them and stopped my bike; I was straddling the seat, my sneakers barely touching the pavement, ready for a quick getaway.

Barry smiled casually. "Hey, Suzy, how're you doing?"

"Oh, I'm great," I said, trying to sound natural.

"Mmm. Well, let me introduce you. Suzy Powers, this is Peggy Timmons."

"Nice to meet you," Peggy said. I nodded and smiled. I couldn't help comparing myself to Peggy. I wanted her to look like a movie star or something, so I could have told myself it was no wonder Barry preferred her to me and shrugged it off. But she was just like any other girl.

She was about five-foot-three, four inches shorter than me. She had short wavy blond hair, a round, freckled face, and blue eyes—nothing really out of the ordinary. And I knew we both felt the same way about meeting like this. It was awful. Barry, however, seemed oblivious to our feelings.

I had to make conversation. "It's been a great summer. Too bad that school starts in a few weeks!"

"Yeah," he said sadly.

For an instant my heart fluttered in hope at his look of dejection. But then he affectionately squeezed Peggy's shoulder, and I realized his sigh was because they'd be in different schools come September.

For what seemed like a hundred horrible years but was more like a minute, the three of us stood there like statues.

Finally I broke the silence. "Well, I've got to run, or I'll be late for my date."

"Sure, Suzy." Barry sounded relieved.

"Nice to meet you," Peggy said again. I hopped on my bicycle, and Barry waved as I rode off.

I pedaled furiously in the direction of home. *That's right,* I told myself. *You don't want to be late for your big date with the "Movie of the Week," do you?*

Meeting Barry—especially with that girl— was a million times worse than I'd fantasized it would be. But Barry hadn't seemed to mind at all.

I hate you, Barry Howell, I thought as I got off my bicycle in the driveway and walked it into the garage. Aloud, I said, "I hate you, I hate you, you'll be sorry one day!"

When I got upstairs and looked in the mirror, I got a big shock. Finally I had to face the truth. I was a real wreck. Ever since Barry had broken up with me, I'd stopped caring about myself. Now, as I looked in the full-length mirror on my closet door, I saw what a mess I'd become. I should have gotten my hair trimmed weeks ago. My bangs were falling in my eyes, and the scraggly ends of my hair were dried and split from too much sun.

I hadn't worn makeup, not even a touch of mascara, in a month. And even though I'd ridden my bike to the library in the center of town, where *anybody* might have seen me, I was wearing the same torn, baggy cut-offs and stretched-out Jefferson High T-shirt I usually wore around the house.

I looked at myself for a long time. Then I straightened up and took a deep breath. Right then and there I decided that I was going to pull myself together—as Donna had been encouraging me to do and as my mother had been subtly urging for weeks. I was not going to let Barry Howell ruin my life. *I am not going to look or act or feel like this anymore*, I vowed to myself. *From now on, I am going to look the best that I can.*

I suddenly decided that I was too young to tie myself down. A girl didn't need a steady boyfriend at my age. *From now on,* I thought, *I am going to have the best time of any girl in the new junior class at Jefferson High School. After all, happiness doesn't mean one boy named Barry Howell.* My new rule was simple: Look great, go out, and meet a lot of other boys.

Chapter Two

It was just two weeks before school started that I made my new resolve. I worked on my tan, biked to keep in shape, cut back on desserts—the works. I used some of my baby-sitting money to get my hair cut, and my mother gave me money to buy a new skirt and a few blouses.

The first day of school, I biked the twelve blocks to campus with a funny feeling in my stomach. I wouldn't be going out with Barry. No sodas after school or walks home with him. But I told myself I didn't care because I was ready for a whole new life.

As I steered my bike into the parking area,

I looked for someone I could stroll casually into the building with. I was in no rush to make an entrance on my own. I chained and locked up at the bike rack. A few kids passed me, laughing and joking together. A gang of guys stood leaning against their secondhand cars—you know, the kind of boys who seem too old for high school and just want to graduate and turn their backs on it forever. They'd be here every morning, hanging out until the final bell. But no one I knew was hanging out this morning.

I lingered at my bicycle as long as I could without feeling like a coward while I searched for Donna's father's little red compact car. But, as usual—even though it was only the first day of school—Donna was late.

Finally, I made my way alone up the path that led to the school steps and the green front doors. And wouldn't you know it? The first person I ran into as I entered the big front hall was Joanie Ellis.

I guess every class has its Joanie Ellis, a girl who's popular even though nobody really likes her much. I think everyone's sort of scared of her. Whenever there's a special committee or a social event, Joanie Ellis ends up in charge. Better to have her for a friend, everybody figures, than for an enemy. Joanie the Phony was what Donna and I called her behind her back, but we were as nice to her on the surface as all the other kids were.

As soon as Joanie spotted me, her blue eyes opened wide, and she headed toward me. She looked as if she'd just discovered a really hot, newsworthy item—me.

"Oh, Suzy! How are you?" she asked, her voice dripping concern. She patted my shoulder compassionately with her free hand. "I was so upset when we got back from Disney World and heard about you and Barry."

My heart thudded. I muttered, "Oh, really?"

"If I hadn't been so busy going into Philly all the time with Mother to do my clothes shopping, I'd have called you. I was just shattered when I heard the news!" Joanie shook her head sadly from side to side.

"That's nice of you, Joanie, but it wasn't necessary," I managed to say, tossing my hair back over my shoulders and looking for someone else to talk to.

"You mean, you're not upset?" Joanie looked at me skeptically.

I forced myself to be cool. "I think it's sort of silly to have a steady boyfriend in high school anyway, don't you? Frankly, I'm glad

I'm not going to miss out on anything this year. I was getting so tired of being tied down."

"Were you?" she asked sweetly. Her pitying smile showed she didn't believe a word I was saying. "Well, I'm just glad that girl Peggy, or whatever her name is, doesn't go to Jefferson. I don't want to have any classes with the kind of girl who'd steal another girl's boyfriend."

I let myself sound irritated. "She hardly *stole* him from me, Joanie. Barry's a person, not a book or a piece of jewelry. And we'd been thinking of seeing other people for a long time." I couldn't stand her prying anymore.

"Oh, I'm so glad you're taking it so well!" she gushed. I could tell she was disappointed because I wasn't giving her a chance to be the comforting friend.

"Joanie, I appreciate it. But I'm OK."

"Really, Suzy." She stared hard at me. Then she turned her head away and said, "Look, there's Lisa Meyers! I've just got to find out if she's trying out for varsity cheerleading with me this year." Waving goodbye, Joanie hurried away.

I heaved a sigh of relief as Donna, her hair flying wildly, bounded through the doors.

Donna always looks like she's on her way to a fire. Give her two hours to get ready to go somewhere, and she'll still discover at the last minute that she's forgotten something.

"Good! You waited for me," she said in a rush. "Hold my notebook for a second, would you? I got dressed in such a hurry, my blouse is half untucked."

"Come on." I nudged her. "Let's get to homeroom before Joanie Ellis comes back oozing sympathy. I've had all I can take of her for one morning."

"Oh, is she just *soooo* heartbroken to hear about you and Barry?" Donna asked, shaking her head so hard that one of the red plastic combs in her thick black hair threatened to fall out.

I nodded.

"Don't pay any attention to her." She pushed the comb back in place. "Let's just hope she's not in Mr. Merrick's homeroom with us."

I followed her, my smile permanently in place, my hellos bright and cheery, my head held high, ignoring the curious stares and questioning glances of some of the girls.

Things didn't go as badly as I'd feared. Nobody, thank goodness, followed Joanie Ellis's example and made a fuss over my breakup with Barry. Even better, Barry wasn't in my homeroom or in any of my morning classes. By the time I met Donna, Ellen Matthews, and Ginny Tompkins in the lunch-room at noon, I was feeling pretty mellow. Suddenly, breaking up with Barry didn't seem like such a big thing at all.

"How's it going?" Donna asked as we filed through the cafeteria line, picking up burgers, plastic dishes of potato salad and rice pudding, and little cartons of milk.

"Not bad," I said. "I've got Mrs. Olsen for chemistry, which is a drag. But having Miss Fielding for American history sort of evens it out."

"My brother had Olsen last year." Ginny reached for an extra dish of pudding. "He said she was an awful stickler. *Very* strict." Catching the disapproving stare Ellen was aiming at her tray, she added defiantly, "Nobody diets on the first day of school."

"Eat whatever you want," Ellen told her. "Only don't come crying to me next time you don't get the part you want in the school play because you're too heavy." Ellen's as thin as a toothpick. She shows it off, too, with tight jeans and sweaters.

She nodded toward her own tray, which

held an apple, some cottage cheese, and melba toast. "If only you could get it through your head that food doesn't have to be fattening to taste good." This was Ginny and Ellen's favorite routine. If her best friend wasn't as thin as a fashion model. I doubt that Ginny would even try to lose weight. But having Ellen around made everybody—even Donna and me, who considered ourselves just the right weight —feel fat.

"Aw, Ellen, do we have to hear this one again?" Ginny sighed as we all sat down at a table.

"Guess what?" Donna said. "I've got that gross Mr. Morris for science." She groaned, sculpting her potato salad into a little cube as she spoke.

"Science isn't your favorite subject anyway, Donna. You should stick to writing," I said.

Donna looked at me. "Right. I'm looking forward to having Mr. Merrick for English. We'll probably be in the same class." Her eyes lit up. "He's going to recommend me for the Jefferson *Journal*. Isn't that terrific?"

"You bet," I said, smiling. Only a select few got to work on the school newspaper. "You know, some of us were supposed to start a bio club this year, but I haven't seen Mrs.

Lewis yet today." Awhile back, I'd decided I wanted to be a doctor, and I figured starting the club would help me get into a good pre-med program in college. Aside from the fact that I love biology.

Ellen pushed her tray away from her. "Lewis is my homeroom teacher. I'll ask when we can have our first meeting. And, Suzy, you know who's in my homeroom—Barry!"

I swallowed hard.

"Is there anyone else you're interested in, Suzy?" Ellen asked.

I was really grateful when Donna saved me from answering. "I'll tell you who I've got my eye on," she said. "Russ Tatum. Boy, do I ever hope he asks me out!"

"You mean it's twelve-thirty on the first day of classes, and you haven't got a date yet?" Ellen teased. "You're losing your touch, Donna."

"Come on, I'm not that bad, am I?" Donna protested, but she was smiling. She knows as well as the rest of us what a flirt she is. "Anyway, I do have one date—to go roller-skating at Wheelerama with Jeff Eakins next weekend. But that's no big thing."

"Why bother going out with some guy you're

not interested in?" Ginny asked curiously. "Isn't that a waste of time?"

"Going out with a boy is never a waste of time," Donna insisted. "It's good to get experience, it's fun, and it never hurts to have guys know you're popular."

"I'm with Donna one hundred percent," I said firmly, at least as firmly as I could. "There are plenty of boys I wouldn't mind dating, believe me. I'm glad I finally have the chance to do it." I didn't really feel that way, but it sounded good, and it got us off the subject of Barry Howell.

"Like who?" Ellen leaned forward, her eyes bright and curious. "I hope not Denny Sullivan. To tell you the truth, I've got a crush on him. We went to the state fair together."

"No, not Denny," I assured her, shaking my head. "But I think he's adorable," I added quickly. The last thing in the world I wanted to admit was that I hadn't looked at Denny or any other boy since I'd fallen for Barry.

But I wasn't let off the hook so easily. "Tell us, Suzy," Ellen persisted. "There must be somebody you're interested in."

That was when I spotted *him* in the food line.

He was of medium height, and medium

weight, with medium brown hair, but even from the other side of the room I could see that he was better than medium looking, with a wide, warm smile and straight nose, a high forehead that a stray lock of hair kept falling over and crinkly eyes. He wasn't gorgeous, but he was cute. I immediately thought of him as looking "comfy."

I went on with my act. I nodded over toward the boy. "That's someone I'm interested in over there."

"Hmm," Ellen said. "I don't blame you."

Four pairs of eyes at our table followed him as he walked to a table at the far end of the lunchroom and joined two other senior guys.

Donna stared across the lunchroom. "Aha! Mike Kelly!"

"Oh, is that his name?" I said.

"Well, I'll tell you about him," Donna said. Thank goodness, she was finally taking over the conversation. "You don't know him because he was new last year, and you were too busy with Barry to notice any other male on the whole earth." Donna shook her head in wonder at the thought that a girl could be unaware of *any* member of the opposite sex. "Besides, he's a year ahead of us, so he wouldn't have been in any of your classes, except maybe study hall."

"Oh, I've seen him around," Ginny said. "He's kind of cute, isn't he? Real shy and sort of serious, I think. He was working as a sales-clerk at Bennington's this summer."

"What were you doing hanging out in a men's store?" Ellen asked. "Trying to pick up unsuspecting males at the tie and handker-chief counter?"

"Very funny." Ginny sniffed. "I was buying my dad a birthday present, and he waited on me."

"I think he looks like just your type, Suzy," Donna said encouragingly.

Frankly, I couldn't see what Mike Kelly and I appeared to have in common other than that we both had two arms, two legs, and went to Jefferson High School.

"I'll try to find out about him, and then we can plot how to get him to ask you out. Oh, don't look so shocked, Suzy. I'll be subtle about it."

"But—" I stopped. How could I protest when I had just said that I was available for dates? "Don't start trying to matchmake, please," I said sternly. "Remember, I'm out to have a good time and see lots of people this year. I'm through with that just-one-boy stuff." I was even beginning to believe it myself.

As we got up and carried our trays to the drop-off window, I took another look at Mike Kelly. He was listening to one of his friends, his chin propped in one hand, his eyes serious and intent. *He looks nice*, I thought.

Chapter Three

I was feeling pretty relieved as I walked into English last period. I hadn't run into Barry all day, and I figured I'd lucked out and didn't have any classes with him. But just at that moment I saw Barry slide into a seat by the door. I quickly took a window seat so that I was as far away from him as possible.

But I couldn't help looking at him out of the corner of my eye. Seeing Barry made me ache. What a cute smile. And he looked fantastic in that red- and white-checked shirt he was wearing; it seemed to make his blond hair shine.

He was busy talking to a couple of his

friends about a boxing match. Watching him gesture and become excited sent a familiar twinge through me, and I guess I got pretty wrapped up in some daydream. I didn't realize how hard I was staring until he suddenly turned around. It seemed as if the whole class watched as we waved to each other. My smile was forced, but I put on a good show. Barry's smile was polite and casual.

Mr. Merrick started explaining class rules and assignments, but I was so distracted I could hardly listen. Why did Barry make me so nervous? I was through with him. I should have been able to put him out of my mind. But I couldn't. I daydreamed my way through class, alternating between fantasies of kissing Barry and of slapping him in the face. Suddenly, class was over, and I hadn't heard a word. I decided to make a quick exit, but Barry and his friends were standing right in the doorway talking. I hung around my desk organizing and reorganizing my books, wishing Barry would leave so I wouldn't have to walk past him. But he was deep in conversation with Russ Tatum and Brent Halsey.

". . . and when he took that left to the jaw, I couldn't believe he didn't go down for the count," Brent was saying. "Well, Cooney has a lot of stamina," Barry replied.

I figured I was stuck. Then I saw Peter Hoffman.

Peter and I had known each other ever since we were both in Mrs. Malling's sixth-grade class together. He was more like a brother to me than a regular guy. I felt safe with Peter, and seeing him now, I was grateful for a friend I could be with.

Peter was gathering up some papers from his desk. I walked over and casually linked my arm through his.

"What did you think of the first day of school?" I asked brightly.

Peter smiled. "Looks like it's going to be tough, Suzy. I'm taking an extra chemistry class."

"I am, too," I replied. "I've got Olsen." I grimaced.

"Maybe we can study together," Peter said.

"That would be great," I said loudly just as we passed Barry and his friends.

"Sure. I've heard Olsen's really tough," Peter was saying as we reached my locker. "I'm glad I got Mr. Moran." I opened my locker and shoved a few books in the back. I smiled at Peter. I felt comfortable with him, and he'd sure helped me through an uncomfortable situation with Barry.

But I was totally surprised when he paused, then asked, "Want to go to the new Clint Eastwood flick at the Corner Cinema?" He added quickly, "Afterward we can stop in at the diner. How does that sound?" He looked at me tentatively as if this were more than a friendship date.

"That sounds fine," I said, although none of it sounded fine at all—not dating, not Peter, especially not the diner. Barry and I had always gone there together.

There's always been a sort of unwritten law about the diner, which is that on Saturday nights it's mostly for couples, though some boys don't mind going there with a whole group of guys. But anyone who goes out on a date on a Saturday night ends up in the diner sooner or later. It doesn't matter that there aren't any video games or that the songs on the jukebox are all at least a year old. The diner is still the place.

, "When do you want to go?" I asked.

"Saturday, say seven-thirty." He looked at me again.

"Fine," I said.

"We'll have to walk. I've been saving for a

car, but I won't have enough money until Easter."

"Oh, that's OK. The Corner Cinema isn't far from my house." I knew Peter was embarrassed that he couldn't pick me up in a car.

He smiled and squeezed my arm. "Great. See you, Suze."

I'd never thought about having an actual date with Peter Hoffman before, but I always enjoyed his company, and I supposed it would be as good a way as any to start dating again.

The rest of the week went OK. My volunteer work at the hospital and having a date to look forward to, kept me in good spirits. All in all, I had to admit that I was glad to be me and glad it was fall, Barry Howell or no Barry Howell. For one thing, I was enjoying my classes so far, all of which promised to be more interesting and challenging than sophomore year's.

Working at the hospital meant a lot to me. It was my chance to help out and also to see what it would be like if I did become a doctor. I'd decided to volunteer the year before, when I started thinking about a medical career. At first the wards had scared me—especially the chronic care facility; it was hard seeing all those sick people. But I had learned how to handle it. This year I felt like a seasoned pro.

Tuesday was my first day back at the hospital—I had taken a part-time baby-sitting job in the summer, so I hadn't done any volunteer work—and I was happy to see that most of my patients had recovered and gone home over the summer. Mrs. James and Miss Peacock, two of the nicest nurses, were still assigned to the wards where I helped out.

As I came in, I hugged them both and told them how much I'd missed them.

"We missed you, too, dear. A few of your favorite patients are still here. Mrs. Jaworski's been asking for you."

"I hope she's doing OK," I said. "What about Carolee?"

"Carolee is doing fine," Miss Peacock said. "Don't worry. You'll see all your friends."

I admired both Carolee and Mrs. Jaworski. Neither of them ever complained; both always appreciated having company, even though Mrs. Jaworski was aging and frail and Carolee had spent most of her life in and out of the children's ward being hooked up to a dialysis machine because of her bad kidneys. I felt I was accomplishing something when I was helping people like them. It was wonderful seeing them again, and the afternoon just whizzed by.

But good as things were, I still hurt like crazy when I thought about Barry. All week, whenever he was around, I couldn't help sneaking glances at him. And I couldn't help noticing that, unlike me, he didn't seem to be faking his happiness at all. *I don't want him back,* I told myself. *I just wish he didn't look so darned pleased with himself all the time, that's all.*

On Saturday Peter came to pick me up right on time, which meant I wasn't ready yet. When I came downstairs, he was busily admiring Patty's new pet turtle and telling my mom and dad about his parents' vacation.

"They got back a week ago, Mrs. Powers. They really loved Maine." Peter stood facing my parents on the couch.

"Where did they stay?" my mother asked as I walked into the living room.

"Bar Harbor, Bay of Fundy—you'll have to come and see the pictures."

"I'm sorry to interrupt, Mom, Dad, but we'd better leave now, or we'll be late." I suddenly felt sort of shy in front of my parents with Peter. It had been so long since anyone but Barry had come to pick me up.

Peter said, "Well, good night, we'll be back on time."

After shaking Peter's hand, my father said, "OK, you two, see you later."

" 'Bye, Dad," I said. My father winked at me as we walked out.

My parents thought this was a real date, even if it was with somebody I'd known since we were little kids. I felt like it was, too. Being around Peter as a pal and having a date with him might turn out to be two different things. I wasn't at all sure how to act.

As we walked to the movies, I looked at Peter, for the first time, as a date. Good looking but not that noticeable, not like Barry. He wasn't a slick talker like Barry, either, but he kept the conversation going. He told me all about a play he'd seen in New York over the summer.

"I love Shakespeare, but you really have to study it to act in his plays."

Acting had always been a passion with Peter, in spite of his shyness. He was one of those people who came alive on stage, and he'd been getting good roles in all the school plays ever since sixth grade.

"I like to see Shakespeare, too, but I don't always understand what's going on," I said.

"You'd learn plenty about plays in general if you joined the play committee. You could work behind the scenes if you don't want to act."

"That sounds interesting. I'll think about it." Peter was always trying to convince me to work on the plays, but I never did. Maybe it would be a good way to meet some new guys.

The Corner Cinema was only eight blocks away, and we arrived quickly. I looked around, trying to scan the crowd as subtly as possible to see if Barry was there, but I didn't spot him. That made me partly relieved and partly disappointed.

The movie was good, and, thank goodness, Peter wasn't one of those guys who think they've got to keep up a stream of dialogue during the movie. He just laughed at the funny parts like I did. From the way he said "Hey, that wasn't bad" when the film ended, I suspected he was relieved he hadn't invited me to a movie that turned out to be terrible.

"Still, even though he was nice and good looking in a tall, bearish way, Peter wasn't for me. Whatever chemistry it is that makes people click, I could tell it would never work for Peter and me. Ginny Tompkins was really much more his type—she had a passion for the theater, too—but Ginny's pretty shy around boys she likes, and Peter's shy, too. So I couldn't see how they'd ever get together.

We talked about the movie as we headed onto Franklin Boulevard and down two blocks to the diner. I couldn't help but wonder if Peter felt as nervous about going in there as I did.

The popularity of the diner is hard to explain, but it's been a hangout ever since I can remember, maybe because the waiters and waitresses are mostly college kids from Franklin Corners Junior College and they can remember how high school juniors and seniors like to sit for hours over one or two Cokes. In any case, they never hassle anyone.

The diner was already crowded when we got there. You could hardly hear the jukebox over the sounds of talking and laughing. We found a booth by the window and ordered some burgers. It was then that we began to feel a little uncomfortable together. Maybe it was from being in public, but we lost the ease we'd felt earlier.

Peter played with the salt and pepper shakers as he looked around. "Seems like everyone is here tonight. Oh, hey, I see Paul. I'll be right back. I have to talk to him." Peter got up and rushed off. "Sure," I said to his now empty seat.

Maybe Peter hadn't been to the diner with a girl before. He was so jumpy. And I felt edgy about possibly running into Barry. What a pair we were. I sat alone and watched everyone coming in.

Joanie Ellis came in with Rich Kramer, her off-again, on-again boyfriend. She looked at me questioningly when she saw me sitting alone. When Peter came back, Joanie looked at me as if I were crazy. I'm sure she thought Peter was no substitute for Barry.

"Well, hi, guys, how are you?" she said brightly, holding on to Rich.

I shifted my attention to her reluctantly. "Fine, Joanie," I said.

Peter spoke up. "We went to the film at the Corner Cinema."

Joanie and Rich seemed totally involved in just looking around. Peter and I exchanged smiles, and he said, "Would you two like to sit with us?"

Joanie seemed startled. "Oh, no, thanks, Peter. Rich and I are going to sit with some of his friends over there." She nodded her head. "See you later."

"That's one person I have to deal with,"

Peter said dramatically. "She's heading the play committee."

"Sounds great," I said sarcastically. "How're you doing with her?"

"Well, she won't let anyone interfere with her authority, and we're having a big problem choosing a play. I think a few of us are going to have to speak to Mrs. Salem."

But I barely heard what Peter had said. Because at just that moment, Barry walked in. Peter followed my glance, and I quickly turned my attention back to him.

"Sorry, Pete." I felt Barry's eyes on me. He slid into a booth across the way with Brent Halsey and Brent's date. Of course, Peggy was glued to Barry's side.

I pushed my half-eaten hamburger away.

"Do you want to leave, Suzy?" Peter looked at me sympathetically.

"No, no, not at all. Why should I want to do that?" I said. I could hear Barry's voice plainly from our table. What an act I was playing. I would have loved to get up and go home right that minute.

But if I left, Barry would see how miserable I was. So I thought the next best thing to leaving was making sure I didn't look devastated by Barry's arrival. I hung on Peter's every word when he was serious, and I laughed uproariously at his jokes. Anybody watching us would have thought I was having a terrific time.

But boy was I glad when it was finally late enough so that I could tell Peter I was due home soon. I should have won an Academy Award for the casual way in which I managed to walk out, giving everyone I knew a super-enthusiastic hello as we walked toward the door. I managed to drawl out an absentminded "Oh, hi, Barry, hi, Brent" when we passed their table. I also flashed Peggy a brilliant smile, which I hoped let her know that being with Barry Howell wasn't everything in the world.

It was only when we were outside that I dropped my mask of cheerfulness. As Peter walked me home, I was silent, forcing what I hoped was a contented smile to my lips whenever he glanced my way. But I was too emotionally drained to try to make polite conversation.

"I had a nice time," he said when we neared my house. Then, after a long pause, he added, in the sort of low tone guys use when they're not sure they're saying the right thing, "I hope it didn't upset you seeing Barry at the diner."

"Of course not," I insisted, all the phony perkiness flowing back into my voice. "That's been over and done with a long time."

"Good." Peter didn't sound as if he believed me for a second. "Well . . ." He hesitated when we got to the door. "We'll have to do it again sometime."

"Sure, Peter. Thanks a lot. I had a good time. See you soon." I went inside, closed the door, and slumped against it. Boy, was I glad to see that evening end!

I took off my jacket and walked to the stairs.

"How was your date, dear?" Mom asked as I passed by the living room.

I poked my head in to where she and Dad were curled up on the couch watching TV. Patty, whose official bedtime was eleven o'clock on weekends, was still downstairs. She was rolled up in a tight little ball sound asleep in one of the club chairs. Dad would have to carry her to bed as he usually did on Saturday nights.

"The movie was great." Then, since I didn't want to risk blurting out that I'd seen Barry, I said, "Guess I'll run up and do some reading before I go to bed."

"Don't stay up too late," Mom called as I went up the stairs.

"Don't worry," I answered. After all, why should I stay up late? There was nothing to do except think about how Barry liked someone else better than me, how he'd finally found the "real thing" at last.

I switched on the light in my room. *This is the room of a girl who couldn't keep her boyfriend,* I thought. I looked around as if I'd find some clue to why Barry had dumped me. But nothing there told me anything. It all looked so normal. The oak headboard and the sea-blue comforter, the bright red wall unit with its built-in desk, bookcases, and stereo stand, even my books and record albums—they were the same things I'd had when I first met Barry.

I pulled off my clothes and dropped them on the desk chair, then pulled on my favorite old flannel nightie. I threw myself on the bed. I was disgusted with myself. Only an old friend like Peter Hoffman would put up with me.

I went to the bathroom and washed my face, and as I looked in the mirror I told myself, "I am not unlovable." Besides, lots of other girls didn't have boyfriends, and they still had a good time. Going out with Peter tonight *had* been OK—at least until Barry appeared on the scene. And any date was better than sitting around moping. If I didn't go out, how would everyone know that I'd gotten over Barry?

Anyhow, I wasn't so sure I'd ever loved Barry all that much. So what was keeping me from making the most of my social life?

Nothing.

I brushed my teeth and vowed I'd stop making myself miserable. I was definitely going to put Barry Howell out of my mind once and for all—even if I had to go out with every boy at Jefferson High School to do it!

Chapter Four

Sunday morning I usually sleep late, but at nine o'clock the little white Princess phone my parents had given me for my sixteenth birthday rang. I keep it on the night table, right near my ear, so I practically jumped out of bed when it rang. I quickly grabbed the receiver.

"Hello," I said groggily.

"Tell all," I heard Donna's voice order.

"Donna!" I glanced at my clock. "It's only nine o'clock."

"Well, *I'm* up." Donna made an unsuccessful attempt to stifle a yawn. "And Jeff and I didn't leave the roller rink until midnight.

42

Then we went to the new place out by the mall for a snack afterward." She yawned again, loudly this time. "But you know why I'm calling, you dope. I wanted to know how your date went. Did Peter Hoffman turn out to be Matt Dillon, Clint Eastwood, and Rick Springfield all rolled into one?"

"Oh, it was all right."

"You sound as enthusiastic as if you were talking about having your tonsils out. I think Peter's nice."

"Oh, he is, he is. It's just that—I don't know, I guess Peter and I have known each other too long to feel romantic."

"And I guess you're still too hung up on Barry to notice anybody else."

"No, it's not that at all. I realized that last night. I'm not in love with him anymore. If anything, I feel sort of *dead* about him, if you know what I mean."

"I'm not sure I do," she admitted.

"Well . . ." I thought it over. "I don't feel a whole lot toward him anymore. I'm not even sure I ever really loved him as much as I thought I did. And I get so mad when I think of what a creep he was about breaking up. I *do* want to go out with other guys, Donna.

But for some reason it's really difficult. Maybe I'm just afraid of being hurt again."

"How about Jack Carlton?" Donna asked. "I heard through the grapevine that he's interested in you."

"He is?" That was pretty exciting, even though I didn't especially like Jack Carlton; who cracked too many jokes. He was one of those guys who made it almost impossible to carry on a decent conversation because he was constantly making puns or breaking in to ask, "Did you hear the one about . . .?" But he was OK, not bad looking in a wiry sort of way, tall and skinny, with a thick shock of dark hair that always needed trimming.

"Jack told Steve Dooley, who just happens to be my date for the Fall Fling, that he was trying to figure out if Suzy Powers would accept if he asked her to double with us."

"And?" I prompted her.

"And I said I couldn't imagine why you wouldn't. I told Steve you were serious about going out with new people and weren't up for getting back with Barry again. Don't worry, Suze, in a few more weeks, no one's even going to remember you used to be Barry Howell's girlfriend."

"I wouldn't mind going out with Jack," I said. Then, hearing how unenthusiastic I sounded, I added, "And it would really be fun to double-date with you and Steve."

"Great! I'll bet Jack asks you tomorrow at school."

"But what about Jeff?" I asked. "Didn't you have a good time with him?"

"Sure, roller-skating's always fun, and Jeff's a neat enough guy. I'd go out with him again in a minute. But that doesn't mean I've got to say no to everybody else, does it?"

"I guess not," I agreed.

"What are you doing this afternoon?" Donna asked.

"Homework." I groaned. "And I wanted to work on the biology club charter. We have to show it to Mrs. Lewis in order to become official."

"Yeah, I've got some reading to do, too. Well, I'll see you in school tomorrow. Wait for me in the morning."

"Sure, Donna. 'Bye." I put down the receiver and looked out on a wet and dreary Sunday. It was a perfect day to study, but I couldn't pull myself out of my glum mood and get to work. What if Jack didn't ask me out? What if *nobody* ever asked me out again?

Or worse, what if I *did* find someone I really liked? A few fun months and then another terrible breakup. I'd just hurt all over again. I sprawled on my bed and forced myself to do some studying. Tomorrow had to be a better day, I thought.

On Monday morning I took more pains than usual with my hair, clothes, and makeup. I figured it was a good way to beat the blues. At least, that's what all those articles on how to get over a broken heart say. Not that I considered my heart broken, but I'd die if I looked like that to everyone else.

I spent a lot of time dawdling in the halls that day, hoping I'd run into Jack. I knew I was looking my best in my new lavender skirt and matching top, but I felt pretty low. Do you know how rotten it feels to be all dressed up and waiting for some guy you don't even really care about to ask you out? I hung out by the drinking fountain and tried to give the impression I was waiting for somebody specific.

It wasn't until a voice behind me asked, "Are you trying to polish that square of linoleum?" that I realized I'd been drawing circles on it with the toe of one shoe.

I whirled around, ready with a sarcastic

remark—and came face to face with Mike Kelly.

Whatever I'd meant to say was forgotten. He gave me a friendly open smile, and he looked so well-meaning and cheerful that I couldn't have said a sarcastic word to save my life.

"To tell the truth, I'm just killing time," I admitted. "Don't you hate to be the first one in a classroom?"

He nodded. "Definitely. Makes me feel as if everybody else who comes is going to accuse me of trying to kiss up to the teacher."

I stood there, a frozen smile on my lips, trying desperately to think of something to say but coming up with a great big zero.

Luckily, he saved the day. "You're a junior, aren't you?"

"That's right," I said. "Suzy Powers. And you must be a senior, right?" I asked, as if I didn't know perfectly well who he was.

"Yep, Mike Kelly. I started here last year when we moved from Chicago."

"Boy, you must think Franklin Corners is duller than dull after living in a big city like that," I said, a little surprised at the way my numbed mind had snapped back and was functioning. "Chicago must be really exciting."

He laughed. "Not really. It's a lot like Philadelphia, only colder. Compared to the wind-chill factor when the breezes come in from Lake Michigan, winter in Pennsylvania's practically tropical. And I like living in a small town. Cities are awfully anonymous, you know."

I didn't get a chance to answer—not that I could think of anything to say anyway that would convince Mike Kelly immediately of my wit, charm, and intelligence—because the class bell started ringing.

"Whoops! I'd better run." He smiled his crooked grin again. "Nice to talk to you, Suzy."

" 'Bye, Mike," I said confidently.

Of course, that confidence lasted no longer than it took for Mike to step around the corner. *What if he thought I was boring?* I worried. I began to think I hadn't said a single interesting thing. *Oh, well, at least we finally met,* I thought as I hurried off to class.

Anyway, I didn't see Jack until the end of the day and then only after a pretty strange incident. I was rushing to my locker after last period when I ran into Barry. It was awful. I literally crashed right into him. I can't explain how weird it felt as he put out his hand to steady me. I was almost in his arms—the same arms I used to feel so safe and happy in. And when he muttered "Sorry, Suze," I could only think that the lips forming those words were the very same lips that used to kiss mine and make me feel so special.

"Oh, that's all right, Barry," I said, pulling away from him abruptly. "It was my fault."

"How are things?" he asked. "Everything all right with you?"

The look he was giving me really made me mad. It was the look you save for people you feel sorry for. As if my life were in shreds because he had dumped me.

"I'm having a great time," I said sweetly. "Really, I never knew being unattached could be so much fun."

Barry looked confused, almost crestfallen by my answer. I waltzed away, feeling his eyes boring into me. I knew he was let down because he wanted me to need him still. But from now on, Barry would have to feed his enormous ego at somebody else's expense, I thought angrily. I was lucky to be rid of him!

"Hey, Suzy Doozy, you look like you're mad at the world!"

It was Jack Carlton, who was leaning against the wall by my locker. Knowing Barry was probably still watching, I flashed my biggest smile. "Nope, Not mad. Just irritated. I almost got knocked down a second ago. The way people career through these halls!" I ignored the fact that it had been my fault.

"And what if I invited you to the Fall Fling?" he asked, trying to be what I imagine he considered sexy. "Would that knock you off your feet?"

"I don't know about that," I answered teasingly. "But I *might* say yes."

"Consider yourself invited then."

"And consider *you*rself accepted."

I continued on down the hallway, smiling like the Cheshire cat. I'd show Barry I didn't need him. By the time I was through, I was going to be the most sought after, popular girl in the whole junior class!

The Fall Fling had all the makings of a romantic evening. The setting was right: the gym was covered with crepe paper, the band was terrific, and the subdued lighting created a wonderful atmosphere. I had on a peach-colored chiffon dress, and I had to admit that Jack looked good in his suit and tie.

As we danced in front of the bandstand, he leaned over and whispered in my ear, "Hey,

Suzy Doozy, you look terrific. I love that dress."
He pushed closer to kiss me.

"Thanks, Jack. You don't look bad yourself,"
I said, moving away from him and trying to
keep the irritation out of my voice. The dance
was so much fun. Too bad I was there with
Jack. It almost spoiled the whole thing for
me. I hoped he wouldn't mind if I danced
with some other guys. "Hey, Jack, I'm kind of
thirsty, mind if I get some punch?"

I didn't owe anything to Jack, I told myself,
as I squeezed through the dancing crowd toward the refreshment table. Besides, I didn't
want anybody—least of all Barry—to think I
was getting hooked up with Jack the Joker.

As I drank a glass of punch on the sidelines,
my eyes wandered over to where Barry and
Peggy were dancing. They seemed so easy
with each other. I've got to admit it, I was
pretty jealous. But why? I knew I didn't love
Barry anymore; I didn't even like him. Then
why did I care so much about making him
think I was having such a terrific time? I was
still living for Barry with this stupid dating
act.

And I couldn't help feeling bitter, too. If
Barry hadn't broken up with me, I wouldn't

be here with Jack Carlton. I *had* to find other guys to dance with.

Just then, Ed Norris walked up to me.

"Hey, Suzy, want to dance?" Ed had been in my biology class the year before.

"Oh, sure, Ed. Where've you been? I haven't seen you in school," I said, as we walked onto the dance floor.

"I know. We don't have any classes together, and I've been busy with football practice."

By the time the night was over, I had danced with quite a few guys and had two dates for the next week.

Everything was working out according to plan. I had just about everything a girl could want: good girlfriends, my two afternoons volunteering at the hospital, parents who were neither too strict nor too busy to pay attention to me, a little sister who was a brat only part of the time, and, I hoped, at least one date a weekend. Then why wasn't I happy?

Chapter Five

The month of October was passing quickly because I was so busy in school. The biology club was finally established. We met every other week, and I was trying to organize a field trip to a research lab before Christmas vacation. I also joined the play committee as makeup artist. And I was dating a lot.

Then, too, I had my friends. I liked the nights when I'd just hang out at a girlfriend's house or when a friend would come over to sit around with me. No date could take the place of the special time I had with my girlfriends.

In the weeks that followed my first encounter in the corridor, Mike and I met by chance every so often. Each time I saw him, I was astounded that I'd never really noticed him before. But that's what going out with only one boy will do to you, I reminded myself. It was as if I'd been blinded to everybody but Barry Howell. But every time I saw Mike, either I was with friends or he was. Sometimes we'd stand in the lunch line together, and then we'd get a chance to have something approaching a real live conversation, but we never seemed to meet alone. There was always a crowd.

I kept telling myself my feelings for Mike were no big thing. He was just another guy, and I had more dates than I could handle already. Of course I hadn't gone out with anyone I cared to see more than two or three times.

One Tuesday afternoon after school, I had just gotten on my bike to go to the hospital, when I heard a deep voice calling, "Hey, wait up and I'll walk with you!"

I turned, and there was Mike Kelly heading toward me, his jacket flapping in the wind.

"Unless you're in too much of a hurry to walk," he added. His smile was so open and warm.

"I'm on my way to the hospital," I said. Then I had to giggle at the look of concern on his face. "Oh, no, no, no! There's nothing wrong with me," I quickly explained. "I do volunteer work on Tuesdays and Thursdays."

"That sounds interesting," he said and really seemed to mean it. "What sort of stuff do you do?"

"Just volunteer work," I swung off my bike and started walking. He automatically reached out and stowing his books in the basket, took the bike and pushed it alongside us. "I distribute library books, play board games with some of the children, write letters for people who can't—a lot of different things."

He gave me a sidelong look that I thought, and hoped, held admiration. "That's a wonderful thing to do. You sound as if it's a pleasure and not a chore."

"Oh, it is!" I was always enthusiastic when I talked about the hospital. "It makes me feel good that I can help people and make them so happy by doing so little. And it sure makes me appreciate my own good health. I mean, other than chicken pox and the measles, I've hardly had a sick day in my life!"

"You're lucky, Suzy." He shook his head, sounding a little rueful. "I'm afraid I was just the opposite. I had arthritis when I was a little kid and spent the better part of three whole years in bed."

"Really? You'd never guess it. You look so healthy!" I exclaimed. I think I blushed, too, when I realized how obvious it must seem from the way I was looking at him that I thought he looked pretty good.

But he didn't seem to notice either my staring or my blushing, and simply said, "Oh, I'm perfectly healthy now and have been for a long time. And in a funny way, I don't regret having been a sickly kid. I read hundreds of books, and I got to think about and understand a lot about life that some people take for granted." He broke off suddenly, and now it was his turn to blush. "Boy, I must sound pretty egotistical, talking like that, and I don't mean to. I just mean—well, there are some benefits to what might sound like a miserable childhood."

The embarrassed redness that rose from his turtleneck sweater and spread up over his cheekbones melted my heart completely. Not only was Mike Kelly cute and nice, he also seemed a whole lot more sensitive than most of the boys I was used to.

"You don't sound that way at all," I assured

him. "I imagine you'd do a lot of thinking, being stuck in bed when all the other kids were out having fun."

"It wasn't a barrel of laughs, that's for sure," he said, grinning again in that special light-hearted way of his.

"I like working with children most of all myself. Even though it breaks my heart that they're in the hospital and that some of them won't ever have normal lives, I like being able to help them. Actually, they're one of the reasons I'm going to be a doctor."

"You want to be a doctor, too?" He stopped for a second and stared at me. "Isn't that funny? I'm hoping to get into Temple's pre-med program myself."

"That's great. I haven't thought about where I want to go to college yet. What made you choose Temple?"

He was silent for a moment and seemed to be thinking about what he was going to say. "For one thing, Temple's a good university," he explained, "and it's got a highly respected medical school. For another, Philadelphia's close enough to here that I could see plenty of my parents. I know it's not going to be easy for them when I leave home."

We were getting closer to the hospital now,

and I found myself walking slower, wanting to prolong every fabulous minute with him. It wasn't just that he was interesting; it was that he made me feel as if I had something important to say, too.

My spirits dipped when, a block from the hospital, he turned the bike over to me and said, "This is where I turn off. My dad is the manager over at the chocolate factory, and I promised I'd give him some help with a few things this afternoon."

"The chocolate factory? Wow! I'm glad my father doesn't work there. My skin would be broken out all the time!"

"Would you believe it?" He raised his shoulders in an exaggerated shrug. "The one thing I'm allergic to is chocolate!"

I laughed along with him. Then, as our chuckles died down, I felt at a total loss for words. For a second I thought about asking him to do something sometime, but the fear that he'd say, "No, sorry, I have a girlfriend," or something, held me back.

And then, almost as if he'd read my mind, Mike stuck his hands in his jacket pockets and, his clear brown eyes meeting mine, said, "If you're free this Saturday night, Bill Chatham's having some people over for a party.

My car'll be out of the shop by then, so I could pick you up."

Words were forming in my mind, but I was so happy that I knew there was nothing I could say that wouldn't sound uncool. I guess Mike took my hesitation for reluctance because he added, "It's not going to be a wild party or anything like that. You can tell your folks Mr. and Mrs. Chatham are going to be home."

Somehow I found an answer that didn't sound overeager. "That would be nice. I'd like to go."

"Terrific." He flashed me another one of his super smiles. "I'll get your phone number before then. And your address, too."

We stood there sort of smiling at each other, saying nothing. Finally, he remembered to gather up his books, and I swung myself onto my bike. "I'd better go. I'm not a doctor yet, so I shouldn't keep the patients waiting."

"I'll see you tomorrow," he said, waving as he turned the corner and walked off down the street.

I waited until Mike was out of sight before I pedaled the rest of the way to the hospital, just in case my legs gave out and I fell down. That's how weak-kneed with happiness I was.

My high spirits were pretty easy to spot, too, because a couple of the patients commented on my mood that day. Mrs. Jaworski, for instance, noticed as soon as I walked into her room. "Don't you look bright and bubbly today?" she said, her crinkly eyes beaming approval.

"Have I been *that* much of a grouch lately?" I asked.

"Of course not, sweetie." She patted my hand as I handed her the library book she'd ordered. "It's just that an old woman like myself can tell when a girl's feeling special. Why, you're smiling as wide this afternoon as if you'd won the million-dollar lottery."

"Nope, not this week," I told her, but I couldn't wipe the grin off my face as I joked, "But then, money isn't everything, is it?"

Of course, when I got home, Patty noticed in a minute and shot a quizzical look at me from where she was sprawled on the living room floor poring over a copy of some preteen movie magazine.

"What are you so smiley about all of a sudden?" she asked.

"You'd think you'd never seen anyone in a good mood before," I said airily as I stepped over her on the way to the TV room.

"Well, you sure haven't been much fun since you-know-who-Howell stopped hanging around," she said smartly.

I could have hit her. I had to remind myself I was sixteen going on seventeen and not eleven. "Who?" I said, my voice rich with puzzlement. "Oh, you mean Barry?" I shrugged as if it were all beneath my notice as I kept going toward the other room.

"Oh, you mean *Barry*? Who? *Barry*?" I could hear Patty mimicking me as I rummaged around for the TV listings. But I wasn't going to let her childishness blur my giddy happiness.

Still, I couldn't even concentrate on the tube because I was thinking about Mike. I tried to figure out why the prospect of a date with him excited me more than the thought of going out with any of the other guys I knew. The more I found out about Mike, the more I appreciated him. He was different from all the other boys I had ever known. He was mature, interesting, and had a sense of humor. I knew he appreciated me and thought *I* might be special. Now, what more could any girl want?

And for the first time since Barry and I had split up, that magical ingredient, chemistry, had come into play. It was there with Mike and me from the start. That's why I felt light-headed whenever he talked to me and why I walked around two feet off the ground after-ward. It was just too exciting for words.

What am I doing wasting my time with reruns of "Happy Days"? I wondered. *I've got to share the news.* I skipped up to my room and dialed Donna.

"Donna, I've got something to tell you."

"Suzy, is that you? What's up?"

"The best. Mike Kelly asked me out!"

"Mike Kelly? That's terrific, Suzy!" She laughed enthusiastically. "He's such a nice guy."

"Mmmm, I know," I answered. "He walked me to the hospital, and we talked about *everything*. He invited me to Bill Chatham's party this Saturday night."

"How did he ask?"

"Well, he had to go help his dad, and I had to rush off to the hospital, so he said it in the last minute. I just couldn't believe it was happening, though. I mean, that he was actu-ally asking me out!"

"Well, I've got a hot date coming up, too. Guess who's going to the movies with Russ Tatum this weekend?"

"He asked you out again!" I squealed with delight. Donna had gone out with Russ for the first time the week before, but at the end of the evening he hadn't asked her out again, and she had been sure he never would. "Oh, Donna, this is fabulous! Maybe we can even double-date sometime. I mean, if we go out with Mike and Russ again," I added.

"*If?*" she laughed. "You sound as if you're really interested in Mike. And I thought Suzy Powers was the one who said she wanted no strings attached. Ha!"

"I *do*," I protested. "Don't get the wrong idea, Donna. I'm not planning to give up my whole social life just because a certain guy has asked me to go to a party with him. I don't think I want to go out with just one guy again as long as I live."

Donna giggled. "Listen to us," she said. "No sooner does somebody ask us out than we start refusing to be his girlfriend. Talk about femmes fatales! But to tell you the truth, I'm glad you're not planning to settle down this year. I think we single girls should stick together."

"You said it! I figure there's plenty of time ahead of me for tying myself down. Right now I wish I hadn't wasted so much time seeing Barry exclusively. No more steady boy-friends for this girl," I vowed. "I'm having too much fun as it is."

"I know what you mean, dahling," Donna said in her most affected, theatrical voice. "It *is* so difficult keeping track of all these scads of men, isn't it?"

We laughed and talked until my mom yelled up the stairs, "Suzy, it's time for dinner, and you've got to set the table tonight."

Donna and I said goodbye, and I hurried down the stairs, still grinning like a fool.

Chapter Six

The party at Bill Chatham's house was lots of fun. Kids filtered into the basement, past Mr. and Mrs. Chatham, who sat in the living room trying to look casually preoccupied and not as if they were chaperoning a party at all. Of course, they found excuses to peek downstairs every so often. Kids danced or sat in little groups talking. There were a couple of juniors there but mostly seniors.

The party was nothing out of the ordinary, but being with Mike was. It was a wonderful whirl, from the time he pulled his rusted old car up to the curb in front of my house to pick me up until he dropped me off a few hours later after the party.

I didn't run right into the house as usual. Instead, we sat in the car talking for at least half an hour. Mike began by telling me about the young doctor who'd treated him as a little boy in Chicago.

"I loved that doctor. He became my friend at the hospital," Mike remembered.

"What was he like?" I asked.

Mike paused as if he wanted to recall every detail. "Well, he was very tall, and he seemed even bigger because I was so little. What I liked most was that he was honest with me. He explained everything. He made me appreciate what doctors could do for people."

"That's really great," I said. "I know some doctors at the hospital who seem very gruff, but when a patient needs them, they're terrific."

Mike asked, "Do you work with some of the younger kids in pediatrics?"

"Yes, all the time. I really visit most of the wards if I can. But pediatrics is my favorite." I smiled. "So tell me, how do you like Franklin Corners?" I asked. I still couldn't believe Franklin Corners could be interesting to Mike after living in a big city. "You really don't find it boring after living in a big city?"

"Not at all, Suzy," he said earnestly. "I like living in a small town. In a big city you're just another face. If I were a senior at my old high school right now, there'd be close to a thousand kids in my class. Instead, there are only two hundred. That means I know almost everybody, and that's important to me. It makes me feel more as if I'm a part of things."

"But kids in Chicago must be so much hipper, more sophisticated and all."

He shook his head. "Not really. Oh, I guess a lot of them are tougher, acting wise and getting in trouble and all. But that doesn't make them any more glamorous. All it means is that if Bill Chatham's party had been held in Chicago, there'd have been a bunch of kids who'd sneak in some six-packs of beer."

"It must look pretty dumb when they take six-packs out from under their jackets."

He shrugged, his broad shoulders rising and falling in the soft glow cast by the street lamp. "I guess some people only get their kicks if they break the rules."

I wrinkled my nose. "I hate beer. I can't see drinking something that tastes like old gym socks have been rinsed out in it."

"You sure look cute when you crinkle up your nose like that," he said in a different, softer tone of voice. "Like a bunny rabbit with bangs."

I started to laugh at his remark, but his lips, soft and sweet on mine, stopped me, and instead of raising one hand to push him away, as I had with all my other dates this year who'd tried to kiss me, I reached my arms up and slipped them around his neck.

When we finally broke apart, I smiled at Mike. "I guess I'd better get going."

Mike said, "How about going to a movie next weekend?"

"I'd love to, Mike. I had a great time tonight." I got out of the car. "Thanks, Mike. And good night."

"Good night, Suzy," Mike said softly.

I unlocked the front door and let myself in. I was nearly dizzy with happiness. In addition to everything else I'd already liked about Mike, he was cuddly and romantic, too. Each kiss had been more delicious than the one before, and when his hands had stroked my hair back from my face, they'd been gentle and caring. I wanted to see Mike again. A lot.

On Sunday my mother asked me to go to the little corner grocery about a quarter of a mile from home. It was one of the few shops in town that stayed open on Sundays. I had just picked up some butter and milk from the dairy case when I saw Donna at the check-out counter.

"Hey, Donna," I called.

"Hi, Suzy! Bring your stuff over."

I walked over while Donna was picking up her bag.

"I had a craving for chocolate chip cookies that wouldn't stop." Donna opened the bag to take out a cookie. "C'mon, I'll walk home the long way to keep you company. I want to hear about the party."

As it turned out, Donna had so much to tell about her date with Russ Tatum that she did most of the talking. I was glad she did. It was too soon for me to tell everything about Mike.

"Are you going out with Russ next week?" I asked as we stood talking under the big fir tree at the edge of my driveway.

"He's so busy he never asks me out in advance, but I'm sure we will. He's picking me up for school tomorrow morning," Donna said.

"Mike asked me out for next weekend," I said happily.

Donna shot me a questioning look from beneath raised eyebrows. "Are you sure you don't want to get involved?"

Why was Donna accusing me as if I had done something wrong? I reacted defensively. "I'd hardly call two dates in two weeks *involved*." I tried to sound cool. "Besides, I haven't said I'm not going to go out with anybody else."

"You mean if some other boy asks you to do something Friday night, you'd say yes?" Donna said.

"Well, sure. Sure I would." Donna's doubts about my following our "no strings" policy had forced me into a corner.

I made my voice as firm as I could. "I'm having too much fun to get stuck with the same guy all the time."

But as I was talking, suddenly all my enthusiasm about Mike was gone. Now I just felt torn between my new feelings for him and my vow to keep things casual.

The next week, my attention was focused on school activities. We'd increased the biology club from every other week to once a week, and I'd already started to work with the makeup committee on the junior class play.

I felt good. My world was beginning to spin again.

Not every minute was exciting, of course. That Friday I spent a full three unexciting hours with Jack Carlton, most of it wondering why I'd ever agreed to go out with him again when I knew perfectly well he bored me.

I guess I wasn't exactly fascinating company myself that night. I got through the evening only by imagining what my next date with Mike would be like, and I didn't pay much attention to Jack. By the time he drove me home, I could tell he was as eager to drop me off as if I'd been a speeding ticket. Strangely enough, I didn't even care. But then, why should I? I had Saturday night with Mike to look forward to—plus I'd already made a date for the following Saturday.

The next night was every bit as wonderful as I'd fantasized it would be. Mike took me to see a double feature at the Corner Cinema, and afterward we went to the diner. Only, this time it wasn't the slightest bit like the night I'd been there with Peter Hoffman. I was so caught up in Mike's company and conversation that I didn't even pay attention to who was going in and out of the front door. I didn't even notice when Barry and Peggy came in. By the time I saw them—sitting in a booth by themselves, the waitress was already clearing away their empty plates.

And I noticed that those two didn't look like they were having much fun. Barry was half-turned in the booth, wisecracking with a bunch of junior guys in back of him and ignoring Peggy, who sat there with a tight, funny smile on her lips. Looking at her, I wondered how many times in the past I'd worn that same expression. Probably more than once, since I could still remember how upset I used to get when Barry talked to the guys and acted as if I weren't there.

Mike was in the men's room when the door swung open again, so this time I checked to see who was coming in. Peter Hoffman. He looked uncomfortable at first when his eyes met mine—I guess that was because this was the scene of our unsuccessful date. But he looked pretty pleased with himself in general, maybe because of the devoted way Ginny Tompkins was hanging on his arm.

Ginny's animated wave when she saw me told me more clearly than words how excited she was to have a date, and I decided then and there I could have been a pretty good matchmaker if I'd set my mind to it. After all, hadn't I imagined Ginny and Peter as a couple? Of course, I never thought at the time that either one of them would work up the nerve to ask the other one out. I was glad to see I had been wrong.

Seeing Peter and Ginny together affected me strangely, though. At least, I guess that's what made me feel vaguely uneasy as Mike and I walked to his car after we left the diner.

Suddenly all my girlfriends were on a dating whirl. Ellen had finally started seeing Denny Sullivan, Donna had gone out with Russ again, and now even Ginny, the shyest one in our crowd, had strutted into the diner on the arm of Peter Hoffman. It was too good to be true in a way. Things were going so well I figured something had to go wrong soon.

I was so poised for disaster that it seemed almost strange that Mike was treating me the same as ever. Finally, after our fifth goodnight kiss, he asked, "Should we do the same thing next Saturday? That Goldie Hawn preview looked pretty funny."

"Sure, I'd love—" I broke off, then asked, "Could we do it Friday instead? I'm afraid I'm busy Saturday night."

Every muscle in my body was tensed for rejection, ready for Mike to tell me to forget the whole thing. Instead, he just smiled and said, "I forgot what a popular girl you are. I don't want you to get the idea I'd take you for granted after just two dates. Friday it is!"

I ran up to the door, literally weak with relief. Mike really liked me. He *did* want to see me again even if I dated other guys. My foreboding had been for nothing.

The next week, nothing could get me down. I flirted outrageously with all the boys, figuring, why not? Now that I was pretty sure the guy I liked best liked me, too, and with no strings attached, I felt pretty self-confident. I could even be nice to Joanie Ellis.

One night, as we were loading the dishwasher after dinner, my mother said, "It's good to see you're back to your old happy self again, Suzy. In fact, you're your old self—and then some!"

As luck would have it, Patty entered the kitchen then, carrying some dirty plates in from the dining room. "That's 'cause she's got a new boyfriend," she announced self-importantly. She gave me a wise old look. "I've seen the way you look at Mike when he comes to pick you up."

"What do you know, twerp?" I retorted, but I couldn't even fake annoyance.

"Oh, brother!" She smacked her forehead.

"Next thing you'll be sitting around all the time, waiting for the phone to ring."

"Don't push your luck, kid," I warned her, an edge creeping in beneath my kidding tone. I guess Mom must have heard it because she quickly handed Patty a mug of coffee and asked her to take it to my dad in the living room.

"Don't mind Patty," she said when we were alone in the kitchen again. "She's probably thinking she'll never be old enough to have dates and boyfriends of her own."

"Boy, if she only knew how complicated her life is going to get!" I exclaimed. "Things were so simple back in the sixth grade."

Mom smiled. "How world-weary you sound, Suzy. Being a teenager isn't all that bad, is it?"

"No, I guess not," I answered slowly. "But it gets confusing sometimes. I suppose one day I'll know exactly what I want, but right now I'm not sure."

Mom looked up. "Do you think being adult is so much easier?" She shook her head. "It's really not, you know."

"But look at you," I insisted. "You never wanted to be anybody but exactly who and what you are now, did you?"

"Of course I did. Why, every time I made a decision, there were other choices I could have made: whether to marry your dad and stay in Franklin Corners or move to Philadelphia to teach there; whether to keep on teaching after you were born or give up my work to be a full-time wife and mother. Life always holds choices, Suzy. We all do the best we can."

"Do you ever wish you'd done things differently?" I asked.

"A few things, maybe. But I can't imagine being happier than I am now, married to your father and having you and Patty. All those decisions didn't make themselves. I had to make them."

I returned to the subject weighing on my mind. "Patty's wrong, you know. I'll never sit around sulking and waiting for another boy to call me again. Not Mike or anybody else." I sighed. "*That's* one decision I've made."

"It sounds as if Mike's turning out to be somebody pretty special in your life. You do like him a lot, don't you, Suzy?"

"He's all right," I admitted, but I couldn't help smiling at my understatement. For once, I was glad when Patty came back into the kitchen and we changed the subject. I didn't want to talk about Mike anymore. Because I *did* like him a lot already, more than a lot. And I was scared.

Chapter Seven

Mike and I changed our minds about the movies and went roller-skating instead on our next date. I couldn't deny how happy I was as we rolled around the rink together, Mike's arm around my shoulders, mine around his waist. I felt that I was where I belonged, next to him. As long as Mike was there, it was as if Barry Howell had never existed.

We skated until we were exhausted. Then we handed in our skates and pulled on our jackets, bracing ourselves for a blast of icy air as we left the rink. I said playfully, "Race you to the car."

"It's a deal!" Mike shouted as I took a head start.

Just as I was sure I'd won, he sneaked up behind me, turned me around, and pulled me tight against him, encircling me with his arms. "Don't you know you can't run away from me?" he murmured. The wool of his jacket was rough against my cheek, his breath making little white clouds in the still, chilled air.

When Mike's lips came down to meet mine, I was swept away by feelings of pleasure and comfort I had never known before.

It was right there, in the parking lot, as we were warming each other from the cold, that Mike said, "I want you to be my girlfriend, Suzy." And my heart jumped.

When Mike saw me hesitate, he said, "I'm not the kind of guy to pretend I don't feel something when I do." With one hand, he tilted my chin, and the eyes that gazed deeply into my own were serious and frank. "And I can't pretend you're just another girl to me, because you're not. You're much more than that."

"Oh, Mike," I whispered. I was thrilled by his gentleness, his sincerity. I couldn't do anything but say, "Yes, I want to be your girlfriend. I do."

The kisses sealed our agreement. We got into the car and drove in silence. In front of my house, we kissed good night. Just as I was about to get out of the car Mike said, "Don't forget *this*, Suzy." I put out my hand, and he dropped his class ring into it.

I closed my hand around it and sighed. "Thank you, Mike. Good night."

"Good night, Suzy. I'll call you tomorrow."

I walked into the house dazed with happiness. After getting into my nightgown, I sat cross-legged on my bed, looking down at the treasure I held in the palm of my hand. I set Mike's ring next to me on the night table. It seemed to wink at me in the light.

My feelings rose to sheer joy and then suddenly dropped. How could this be? Had I been too rash in committing myself to Mike? Just a few weeks ago I was determined to have only no-strings-attached dates. No strings, no breakups, no hurt. Now I'd accepted Mike's ring. What had I gotten into?

On Saturday morning I canceled my date for that night. I didn't know what else to do. I didn't feel right about going; yet, when I hung up the phone I began to realize how serious the commitment to Mike was. And I didn't know if I could handle it.

On Sunday Donna came by, and we went up to my room to play records. I didn't even mention the ring. I had tucked it away in the blue-velvet-lined jewelry box on top of my dresser. I couldn't put it on yet. I couldn't tell anyone.

Donna sprawled across my bed. "How was roller-skating Friday night?" she asked.

"It was OK," I answered. "Not too many kids from Jefferson were there, though. I guess the cold weather kept them at home."

"How could you be cold with a hunk like Mike to keep you warm? If Russ had asked me out Friday night, I'd have gone if there was a blizzard!"

I spotted tears welling up in her eyes. "What's the matter?" I asked. "It's not as if you never see him. You had a date last night. Did you two have a fight?"

She shook her head. From the way she was sniffling, I knew she could really break down. "Come on," I prodded her. "Maybe you'll feel better if you talk about it."

"Oh, he's just so maddening!" she blurted out at last. "Russ Tatum's the kind of guy who turns women into confirmed spinsters."

"Come on, he can't be that bad!"

"Oh, no? What would you do if a guy told you he didn't want you to go out with other boys, even though he wasn't willing to see you more than one night a week? And some weeks not even one night. He's making me crazy, Suzy!"

I was mad at Russ for hurting Donna. "You mean he wants to play the field but expects *you* to be faithful?"

She shook her head again. "No, it's not that. It's all those sports he's into. Basketball two nights, bowling one night, hockey practice." She snorted. "Take it from me—never fall in love with a jock!"

"But I thought you didn't want to go out with someone exclusively, anyway," I reminded her.

"I didn't—until I started seeing Russ. What's the use of being someone's girlfriend if you barely see him outside of school? Oh, Suzy, I'm so miserable I can hardly think straight anymore."

I couldn't believe Donna was changing her attitude about boys so drastically.

"Does he feel the same way about you?" I asked. I wanted to help clear up the confusion churning inside her.

She stared at me from tearful eyes. "When we do see each other, we have a great time. I know—I just *know* he cares about me." She laughed bitterly. "Fat lot of good that does me, huh?"

"What are you going to do?" I asked. My eyes were on Donna, but my thoughts were on the jewel case across the room.

"I can't stand this anymore." Donna's voice broke. "I'm going to stop seeing him," she said tightly. "If he can't give up a single thing for me while he expects me to be there whenever he wants me, it can't work out." She sighed heavily, and her shoulders slumped as if she'd breathed out every bit of hopefulness. "You sure knew what you were talking about after Barry broke up with you. I'm never getting involved again. It's too confusing."

My old fears about a steady relationship came back. Donna was right. Russ *was* being selfish, just like Barry. I reached the inevitable conclusion. You can't trust guys. So what was I doing with Mike?

Donna left a little while later, turning down Mom's invitation to stay for supper so she could finish her homework. As soon as she left, I took Mike's ring from its hiding place and slipped it into the coin compartment of my wallet. I knew what I had to do.

I wanted to call Mike at that moment, but I remembered that he'd gone up to Harrisburg with his folks to visit some old family friends. It was dinner time, and he surely wouldn't be back until midnight. So it would have to wait until Monday morning.

I spent that night studying in my room. I tried not to think about Mike anymore.

Monday morning, I awoke feeling tired and achy all over, but I couldn't fool myself into believing I was coming down with the flu or a cold. I knew perfectly well what was wrong with me. I hated having to face Mike, or rather, to face returning his ring.

I knew he'd be at the door to pick me up for school soon. Not just because I was his girl, but, as he said, "It's too cold for you to keep riding your bike every day."

I took a long shower, then slipped into a skirt and sweater. It was only eight o'clock in the morning, but already the day was too long.

Downstairs I poured myself a glass of orange juice and took it upstairs to sip while I did my makeup. The last thing I felt like doing was facing everyone at the breakfast table.

Have you ever felt as if you were two people at once when something was happening? That's how I felt as I walked toward Mike's car. One Suzy Powers was ambling down the walk to the old car at the curb. *That* Suzy Powers could smell the dankness of damp, dead leaves in the air, hear the last few birds of late fall chirping to one another, run a gloved hand through her hair to push it back over her shoulders. The other Suzy Powers sort of floated above, watching and wondering how that girl could possibly act so normal.

I got into the car. I must not have looked so normal to Mike, though. He shifted into drive and pulled slowly away from the curb, but his eyes didn't leave my face until he had to look straight in front of him to steer.

"You look like you've lost your best friend," he commented after he'd grazed my cold cheek with his lips. "You're not mad because I didn't call you last night, are you? It was past twelve by the time we got home from Harrisburg."

"No, it's not that." I tried to say more, but no words would come. Instead, I reached in my purse and took out Mike's ring. It sat balanced on my palm like a fat, frozen teardrop.

"I—I can't keep this, Mike," I told him. "It just doesn't feel right."

He took one look at what I was holding out for him, then pulled the car to a stop. But he made no move to take the ring. He simply looked at me, his face a mixture of puzzlement and hurt.

"You don't want to wear my ring?" he said slowly. "But—why didn't you say so the other night?"

"I don't know." My voice sounded tiny with shame and discomfort. "It—it seemed like I wanted it then, I guess."

"And now?" His voice was even, but the fingers that reached out to take the ring from me were trembling slightly. "What happened to change your mind from one day to the next?"

"Nothing happened, Mike. It's just that—" I *couldn't* explain the hurt I'd been through. I only knew I couldn't go through it again.

"Just what? Come on, Suzy. You at least

owe me an explanation. You make me feel like I'm some sort of creep. Do I have bad breath or something?"

He was trying to make a joke out of it, but it didn't come off. I was divided between my feelings of love for Mike and my fear of getting involved again and possibly being hurt. I reminded myself, *Think how you felt when Barry told you he didn't want to go out with you anymore. Don't make Mike feel bad like that.*

"It's got nothing to do with you, Mike. It's me, one hundred percent *me*. If I were going to have just one relationship, there's nobody else in the world I'd rather go out with than you. But I don't want to, and that's all there is to it." The sound of my heart thudding seemed to pound in my ears.

"What made you decide this?" He slid his ring back on his finger and leaned back. Sitting in the car with him where he'd given his ring, where we'd kissed, overwhelmed me. I had to blink my eyes to stop the tears.

"I didn't decide it, Mike. I've felt that way ever since Barry and I split up. I decided I didn't want to date anyone exclusively. I *still* don't want to tie myself down. It's just that I—I guess I got carried away the other night."

"I guess I did, too. I mean, I actually thought you really wanted to be with me, that you felt the same way I did."

"I do! Or at least I think I do. Look, Mike," I went on, feeling desperate as I saw the stony look on his face, "I like you better than Barry, better than any guy I've ever met. But I don't want another intense relationship. I want to feel *free*."

"What does that mean, Suzy? It's been a few months since you broke up with Barry. If you're not ready now, you might never be."

Angrily he started the car. We drove the rest of the way to school in silence. Mike's face was grim as he pulled into a space and killed the motor.

"Maybe some people weren't just made for going out with one person," I said lamely, no longer able to remember all my reasons against it.

"Or maybe some people were only made for going out with Barry Howell?" he suggested. We got out of the car and headed for school. His voice was softer now. "Is that it, Suze? Are you still in love with him?"

"Of course not. Barry's nothing to me. I don't know what I ever saw in him. I just—"

"Just don't want to see me anymore?" Mike said.

My heart almost stood still at that. I couldn't imagine not dating Mike! That had never occurred to me at all. I tried to tell him that, to assure him that I still wanted to see him, that I wasn't trying to end everything.

"Let me get this straight," he said quietly when we were inside the building. He leaned against the wall and looked down at me. All I could wish was that he'd never asked me to wear his stupid ring in the first place, that everything could go back to being the way it had been before Saturday night. But it was too late for that. There's no way to turn back the clock.

"You don't want a steady relationship." Mike was saying, "but you don't want to stop seeing me, either. What do you want me to do, Suzy? Share you with other guys?"

"It sounds awful when you put it that way," I protested. "We'd still be special to each other. But we wouldn't have this heavy-duty commitment hanging over our heads." Tears were forming in my eyes again. "Please, Mike, give it a chance. Everything will be the way it was, you'll see."

The misery in my voice must have reached him because his arm slid around my shoulders. When he spoke again, he didn't sound mad anymore. But he didn't sound as if he agreed with me, either.

"I don't know if it *can* be the way it was before," he said slowly. "I know what I need, Suzy. I don't want to date anybody else—I want you to be mine." He bit his lip. "That means everything's changed. I don't know if I can stand watching you date other guys."

The bell for homeroom rang then, saving me from having to say something, from having to plead with him to try it my way. His arm slipped off my shoulders. He shrugged and tried to smile. "Look, Suzy, I'll give it my best shot, OK? But I can't promise anything. I mean, my idea of having a girlfriend doesn't include her dating my friends."

"I don't even know if I want to date anybody else right now," I said, trying not to shout over the voices of the kids who were filing through the corridor. "I only mean I don't—"

"Don't want a heavy commitment," he finished for me. "OK. We'll try it your way. For a while."

He ruffled my hair and walked away. I rushed to my homeroom, so late I'd have to ditch my jacket and switch books at my locker before my first class. I was weak with relief as I sank down on the chair behind my desk. I'd gotten my way! Now everything was going to be all right. I still had Mike—with no strings attached—the way I wanted.

Chapter Eight

I don't know how I fooled myself into thinking everything was going to work out fine. I guess I wanted so badly for things with Mike and me to be all right that I didn't give myself a chance to think about it.

The first week, everything was pretty much the same as usual. I went to school, had a few class play meetings, caught an early movie with Ellen and Donna one night, and did my volunteer work at the hospital. Mike still drove me to school, and I went to the diner with him for hot chocolate one afternoon after school. I liked seeing him more often than I had when we'd first started dating, and I saw no reason to pretend that I didn't. What I didn't want was . . . well, to have no one to fall back on if things didn't work out between Mike and me.

That Friday night I had a date with Tom Shaw, a friend of Denny Sullivan's. Ellen was dating Denny pretty steadily now, and we doubled with them. That was one reason I'd accepted when Tom asked me. The other reason was that I wanted to remind myself I was still a free agent.

"You went out with Tom? I think you're crazy." Those were Donna's words on the subject Saturday afternoon as we took the bus to the mall to shop for winter boots. When we stopped for milk shakes at a little ice-cream shop there, I finally confessed to her that Mike had given me his ring and I had given it back.

"What would you have done in my place?" I asked Donna.

"I'd have put his ring on a chain around my neck immediately. And stopped seeing other boys, of course," she said. "That's what I'll do if Russ gives me his ring."

"I thought you were through with Russ. That's what you said last week, Donna."

She smiled guiltily. "Don't you know better than to believe everything I say? Russ and I talked it over last night, and he's agreed to spend less time being a jock and more time with me. At least he's not fooling around with other girls."

"I can't understand you." I felt she'd betrayed me somehow. "You and I were going to be the girls who didn't get stuck in exclusive relationships, remember? Even if you don't have Russ's ring, you're letting yourself get tied down. Do you mean you'd honestly say *no* if another boy asked you out?"

"Yes, I would," she admitted after thinking it over. "I wouldn't want to take the chance of losing Russ."

"But you said . . ." I could feel anger and confusion rising.

"I know, I know. I said I liked being single. But don't you see, Suzy? That's because there wasn't anyone I really liked then. Now I've got Russ. I *like* being his girlfriend. Why see anyone else if you've got one guy who makes you happy?"

"Why not?" I argued. "Think of all the chances you're letting slip by, all the fun you're missing!"

"What fun? Wouldn't you rather have seen Mike last night?"

"That's beside the point. The point is that

it's silly to live like a settled old couple when you're still in high school. I thought we agreed on that."

"I changed my mind." Donna sucked up the last drops of her chocolate shake with a loud slurping noise she knew I hated. That's why she always did it. She pulled out her wallet. "C'mon, let's pay for these and go to the two shoe stores down at the far end of the mall. Ginny bought her maroon boots at one of them, but I can't remember which."

"OK," I said unhappily. Donna's observation had jangled me more than I'd admit to her. Because she was right. I'd much rather have been with Mike the night before than with Tom. But I still thought it was safer to see lots of guys than to limit myself to one.

That night, when Mike came to pick me up to go to the diner, I had a sinking suspicion that something was wrong. I didn't want to ask him point-blank—I was afraid he'd tell me something I didn't want to hear—but it was hard to ignore his mood. He said barely two words to me as we drove.

"A penny for your thoughts," I murmured when we pulled up to the curb a short ways from the diner.

"That's almost as original as 'Cat got your

tongue?' " he said, in a tone of voice I'd never heard from him before, not sulky, but faraway and detached. Then he smiled apologetically. Sounding more like his old self, he said, "Don't mind me tonight. I guess I'm just in a weird mood."

I accepted his explanation and told myself that I wasn't what was getting him down. Inside the diner, though, it was impossible not to see that Mike was different. He went out of his way to table-hop or to call other kids over to our booth to chat. I'd have had to be blind not to notice. Gradually, a gnawing sensation in the pit of my stomach told me there could be only one reason Mike was acting the way he was: for some reason, he didn't want to be alone with me.

The ax fell as soon as we were back in the car again. "Want to cruise over to that new place and see if anyone's hanging out?" I asked, desperate to prolong our date. "You know, the one over by the mall?"

The question hung in the air while he started the engine. "I don't think so," he answered, his voice low. "I'm pretty beat."

"OK." It came out in barely a whisper as I sat scrunched up on my side of the car, not daring to say anything more, preferring utter, uncomfortable silence to what I was afraid might be coming next.

He didn't even wait until we got to my house to say it. He wanted to get it over with quickly, like I did when I'd returned his ring.

"I've given it a lot of thought, Suzy," he began as he drove. He sounded even more far away than before. "I can't go on this way. I know you went out with Tom Shaw last night. I don't care if he doesn't mean a thing to you or if you're crazy about him. The fact is I can't stand thinking of you as my girlfriend and then hearing about how someone ran into you with another guy. So—so I think we shouldn't see each other anymore."

My heart sank. "But you didn't even give it a chance," I protested.

"Don't you understand, Suzy?" His voice was impatient, almost angry. "I don't need to give it a chance. I know how I feel. The last thing in the world I'd do is pressure you into seeing me exclusively when it's not what you want. But having a steady relationship and *not* having one at the same time—it's not what *I* want."

"But—but we're too young to have a steady relationship!" I cried.

He laughed bitterly. We were at my house,

and he stopped the car. "No, Suzy, we're not too young. Getting engaged, getting married—sure, that's for older people. But going out with only one person *is* for people our age. Since I want to and you don't, it seems to me our heads are in two different places."

"And never the twain shall meet," I said sadly. If he felt this way, I couldn't argue anymore. I slid farther from him on the seat and swung my door open. "Well, I guess it's best that we got things settled. Of course, there's no hard feelings on my part. You're perfectly right, Mike. I guess our heads aren't in the same place at all."

With that, I jumped out and closed the car door, being careful not to slam it. I had my pride, and I wasn't about to advertise how angry and upset I felt. *Guys,* I thought blackly as I walked to the front door, *they're all alike underneath. All they really care about is what they want.*

I let myself in quietly, but not quietly enough. I could hear Mom and Dad talking in the living room when I slipped through the hall. No sooner had I hung my jacket on one of the pegs in the hallway and gone to the kitchen to pour myself a glass of fruit punch than my mother followed me in.

"My, you're home early tonight!" She tried to sound surprised to see me, but I heard the worry in her voice. "Your father and I walked in a few minutes ago from the Hoffmans' little get-together." She stood there uncertainly while I drank the punch and rinsed out the glass.

"Some nights nothing much is happening, you know?" I said casually.

She came right out with it, not hiding her concern any more. "You and Mike didn't have a fight, did you, dear?"

"Of course not!" I snapped. Then I wondered why I should take out my anger on Mom. "We've been seeing too much of each other, Mom," I said in a softer tone. "When you do that, you don't always have a lot to say to each other."

"But isn't it nice to spend some quiet time together?" she asked, relieved now that she thought everything was OK.

"Mmmm, sometimes," I agreed half-heartedly, the memory of Mike's few words—more awful than any long conversation—still fresh in my mind.

Mom stood there waiting for me to say more. Then she opened the door of the refrigerator. "I came to get your father a beer."

"Well, I'm going to go up and sort my laundry before I go to bed." I tried to ease my way out. "I'd better do a load tomorrow if I want to have anything to wear to school next week."

"Oh, by the way, guess who was at the Hoffmans' house while we were there?" I shrugged, uninterested. "Your friend Ginny Tompkins. You didn't tell me she and Peter were dating."

"I didn't know they still were," I told her honestly. "I saw them together once or twice, but Ginny hasn't mentioned him, so I figured it was all over."

"They seemed to be quite taken with each other," she went on. Mom always uses old-fashioned terms like that when she talks about romance, which she even calls "courtship" sometimes. "Peter tells me they've both got good roles in the play next week. You're doing the makeup, aren't you, dear?"

I mumbled an affirmative, then hurried out of there before Mom could tell me what wonderful relationships my other friends were having. Why was my life the only one that seemed to be all messed up?

Maybe if I'd been able to cry when I was alone in my room, I'd have felt better. But tears wouldn't come. Why should I be upset?

I asked myself. Wasn't *I* the one who'd backed off from being Mike's girlfriend? Only when I made *my* decision, it hadn't occurred to me Mike would make one of his own. But the whole thing was out of my hands now. Mike was out of my life.

I sat and stared at the phone next to my bed for the longest time. Every muscle and nerve in my body told me to pick it up, call Mike, and tell him that I didn't really mean it, that I wanted to be with him and didn't care about going out with anyone else.

But something stopped me.

For one thing, I wasn't about to let Mike blackmail me into doing something I didn't want. For another, no matter how I felt about him, I couldn't wear his ring. I just couldn't!

"Boy, are you a mess, Suzy Powers!" I said to my reflection in the bathroom mirror, while I washed off my makeup and got ready for bed. "Now you're free to do exactly what you said you wanted. You're going to have a ball this year!" I said sarcastically.

I got into bed, and as I slipped beneath the covers and pulled the blanket over my head, I felt miserable, lost, and alone.

Chapter Nine

Monday morning, snow flurries as fine as ashes were drifting from a sunless sky. I got up wearily and shivered as I pulled on a turtleneck and jeans. I couldn't ride my bicycle in this weather, I thought, when I went down to breakfast.

"Good morning, Dad. Hi, Mom," I murmured and took my place at the table.

"Hi, dear," my mother said. "How about some eggs this morning?"

"Well, I'll have time if Dad will drop me off at school." I peeked at my father over his newspaper.

My father looked up from the newspaper.

"Sure, I'll drop you off, Suze." Then a look of confusion passed over his face. In spite of his graying hair and horn-rimmed glasses, he suddenly seemed more boyish than distinguished. "But what about this guy you've been seeing? Mike. I thought you were going to drive with him to school from now on."

My throat felt paralyzed. My mother noticed my hesitation and helped me out.

"Maybe Suzy would rather find her own ride than depend on a friend, darling," Mom said quickly. I could have hugged her. She knew something was wrong, but she'd never badger me to find out and wasn't letting Dad put me on the spot.

Dad's eyes met hers, and an unspoken message passed between them. "Of course I'll give you a ride, Suzy. In about ten minutes."

I sighed in relief. "Thanks, Dad."

Back in my room, I gathered my books and took a last look at myself. I needed something bright to perk me up. My jeans and tan turtleneck needed color, not to mention my own spirits. I combed my jewelry box for the little red enameled rosebud pin Donna had given me last year for Christmas, but it wasn't there. Of course that made me want to find it all the more. I rooted around in my dresser drawers

103

until my fingers touched something cool. I reached in and pulled out the framed picture of Barry I'd stuck there after I'd sent his ring back to him.

I gazed at it. "To Suzy, with love forever, Barry." *Some forever*, I thought, as I dumped it back into the drawer. But I had to admit life had been much simpler when I was going out with Barry. At that very instant I'd have given anything if we had never broken up.

I was silent as we drove to school. " 'Bye, Dad, see you later," I said as I hopped out of the car.

"OK, honey, see you later."

Donna was just climbing out of her dad's car, too.

"What's up?" she asked. "I thought Mr. Right was driving you to school from now on."

"Well, he's not. Actually," I admitted, "I don't think I'm going to keep seeing Mike." This was as good a time as any to get it out in the open.

"What!" She stopped dead in her tracks, despite the cold air and the steadily falling snow. "Not at all?"

"I'm not sure. Mike can really be a drag sometimes, and I'd rather have a good time than a steady boyfriend." I plunged ahead with my version of the situation.

"You mean you're giving him up completely just so you can keep dating?" She looked puzzled. "Well, I guess there's something to be said for sticking by your principles."

We walked into the school building. Donna brushed the snow from her coat and unzipped it.

"It's not only a question of principle, silly!" I went on to explain. "It's a question of wanting to have fun instead of getting in a rut."

"I should be in that kind of rut with Russ," she said dreamily. The final bell rang, and we both had to run. "Suzy, see you at lunch. We can talk more then, OK?"

"OK," I said. "And Donna"—I touched her arm—"don't make a big thing of it, huh?" I lowered my voice. "It's not as if we broke up or anything. We weren't ever really going together."

"Sure, Suzy, see you at lunch."

I saw Mike in the hall between classes, and we acted like old friends. That was fine with me. I hated to think there'd be any bitterness between us.

Donna was saving me a place in the cafeteria line when I got to the lunchroom. "Ginny and Ellen are already over at the table," she told me as I stepped into line behind her. She lowered her voice to a whisper. "So? Have you seen Mike?"

"Sure. I ran into him in the hall," I answered nonchalantly. Suddenly I got very busy reading the big lunch menu that hung on the wall behind the counters. "Boy, big choice! Lamb stew or chicken goulash. I'd kill for a sloppy joe."

"You're out of luck. But the goulash doesn't look bad. That's what Ellen and Ginny got. Oh, by the way"—she went back to her conspiratorial tone—"don't mention Denny in front of Ellen. He's asked Lisa Meyers out for Friday *and* Saturday night this week. I imagine she's sort of upset about that."

I nodded, feeling bad for Ellen. But this seemed to prove I was right to refuse to go out with just one guy. It was much safer.

"What's the story on Ginny and Peter Hoffman?" I asked. "She's been really quiet about seeing him, but my mom told me she was over at the Hoffmans' with him the other night."

"You know Ginny." Donna made a face as she picked up a plate of watery strawberry Jell-O with fruit. "She'll talk a mile a minute about stuff that's not important, but as soon as something big happens, she turns into a clam. But she *has* let it slip a few times that she's been with him. I know they spend a lot of time together during play practice, but now it looks as if they'll still be an item after the play this Friday."

"That's great," I said, trying to muster up some enthusiasm as we maneuvered across the crowded lunchroom.

"And," Donna added facetiously, "Russ has kindly consented to give up bowling that night to take me to the play."

"That's nice of him. And I know *you* wouldn't miss the party afterward." I always kidded Donna about her love of parties.

"You bet. Even though it's only at the diner, I can't wait."

The week passed quickly. I had to attend two dress rehearsals to work on makeup. Friday night was the performance. I was also busy putting myself back into circulation. I hadn't been dating as many other guys since I'd started going out with Mike, and now I didn't want anyone to get the idea I was spoken for. I already had a date with Jeff Eakins for Saturday night.

Two interesting things happened that week.

The first was at the hospital. Mrs. Jaworski seemed eager to talk when I stopped by her room. "How are you, sweetie?" she asked in her gentle, quaking voice. "You've been buzzing around so busily lately, we haven't had much of a chance to talk."

"Oh, I'm fine, Mrs. Jaworski," I answered brightly, a twinge of guilt nagging at me. How could I have been so busy with my own thoughts that I'd ignored this friend to whom company meant so much?

She peered at me craftily from beneath her wrinkled eyelids, her blue eyes bright as a bird's. "You sure you're so fine?" she asked. "You certainly do seem to be bright and bubbly, but you look a little peaked. I thought maybe you were sad and covering it up."

"Things haven't been all that great lately," I said. "I've had a lot on my mind."

"And a lot of boys hanging around, I'll bet." She chuckled. "Well, a pretty girl like yourself should enjoy her youth."

"That's exactly what I've been doing," I announced emphatically.

"Oh, I can recall when I was your age," she reminisced. "What a time I did have!"

"I'll bet you had a lot of boyfriends, didn't you?" I asked. Mrs. Jaworski was older than my grandparents (I'd seen one of her charts in the nurses' station and knew she was close to eighty), but by her delicate porcelain skin and small, perfect features I could tell that she had once been a great beauty.

She smiled. "Oh, I had my share. Of course, I met Will, my husband, when I wasn't much older than you are now, and after that I guess I didn't have eyes for anybody else."

"You mean you got married when you were my age?" I asked, shocked.

"No, I married when I was twenty. But I met Will when I'd just turned seventeen, and after that, I wasn't interested in anyone else."

"But didn't you want to experiment?" I asked.

"Experiment?" She shook her head. "You'll have to explain what you mean, dear."

"Well, didn't you want to go out with other boys even though you liked Will? You know, in case he wasn't the right one. Were you that sure?"

"Wasn't sure at all." She closed her eyes, and I could tell she was far away, sixty years earlier, reliving those precious memories. "I wasn't any different from other girls my age. One minute I wanted this, the next, I wanted that. One day I couldn't imagine being with anyone but Will, next day, I'd worry I was missing out on something and tell him to go away. Oh, I led him a merry chase!"

"So what happened?" I asked eagerly.

"Love happened, I suppose. One day I woke up and admitted that I didn't give a darn about any of the other boys I knew. I was happiest with Will."

"But what if he'd turned out to be the wrong one?"

"Why, then I wouldn't have married him, of course. But as it turned out, he *was* the one. He went away to school, and every time he came home for vacation, we fell more and more in love. Finally, it made sense to become man and wife. We had almost half a century together before Will was taken from me, and there wasn't one minute I regretted." Her voice was soft and low.

I put a pillow under her head and said gently, "Do you need to rest, Mrs. Jaworski?"

She murmured, "Yes, dear."

A moment later, the regular deep sound of her breathing told me she'd already fallen asleep. I tiptoed away, trying to envision the white-haired man with the mustache and double chins as a romantic, impetuous suitor. His photograph held a place of honor on Mrs.

Jaworski's nightstand, set in a circle of other photos of children, grandchildren, and two great-grandchildren. I couldn't picture myself spending fifty years with anybody. But I knew people did it all the time. My own parents had been married twenty-three years.

The sentiments Mrs. Jaworski had expressed stayed with me all afternoon. I tried to understand how they applied to my life. I knew I wasn't ready to make a commitment. I understood that wearing Mike's school ring wasn't the same as marrying him, but I still didn't want to do it.

The other thing that happened took place Friday night after the class play. Everyone involved with the play was showing up at the diner. We had decorated the diner earlier in the day with crepe paper and set up tables so we could all sit together in one group. The tables in the back were half-filled by Jefferson students, and others were filtering in. We play people were happy to be together having fun after all the work we'd done in the last week of rehearsals.

Then Donna came in with Russ, and they stopped by to say hello to us. "Suzy, the makeup was great," Donna said.

"Well, don't give me all the credit. Everyone

here worked for it." I waved my hand around the table.

Donna bowed her head. "Congratulations, all. Now, I'm going to congratulate the stars." Donna and Russ walked over to Ginny and Peter, who were sitting at the main table.

Ellen came in a little while later with Brent Halsey. She looked like a prima ballerina, with her wisp of a body and her hair twisted in a little knot.

"Ellen," I called, "come and sit here." She was walking toward me when suddenly I felt somebody plop down beside me. I swallowed hard, thinking it might be Mike. I saw Ellen's eyebrows shoot up in surprise, and she gestured to indicate she was going over to Donna's table. Then I turned to find Barry sitting next to me!

"Hey, Suzy, how's it going?" I looked at him in shock. How could he talk to me so casually after what had happened between us? His perfect white teeth gleamed as he smiled that lazy smile of his and slid his arm up around the back of the booth, the same way he used to when we were seeing each other.

For the first time since we'd broken up, I

was determined to talk easily. "I'm fine, Barry," I answered. "How are you?"

"Good. Great. The play was terrific, huh?"

The jerkiness of his speech told me he was a little nervous even though he was too cool to show it in any other way. His awkwardness gave me confidence.

If he wanted to make small talk, I would, too. "We all did a terrific job. Didn't Peggy come with you?"

"Naw, she's—well, she—" He paused and looked down for a moment. "She and I aren't hanging out much together anymore."

"But weren't you going together?" I asked. I wasn't going to let him off the hook that easily, after the way he'd treated me. My heart pounded when I realized he was here because Peggy probably had dumped him. Yet, his nearness and the familiarity reminded me of when we used to be together. I was softened by those memories and by his vulnerability now.

"Yeah, we were going out, all right. But it's over," he said. He looked off into space rather than meet my eyes.

I couldn't help saying, "You got tired of her already! You're a real heartbreaker," I added in a low voice.

"*I* didn't get tired of *her*," he said, ignoring what I was trying to imply. "If you really want to know, Peggy wanted to go back to her old boyfriend. She never really loved me. I wouldn't be surprised if she only wore my ring to make him jealous."

I almost felt sorry for him, he looked so miserable. But what he had done to me flooded back into my mind. The chance to say it was too tempting. "That's how it goes," I said, patting his hand in mock sympathy. "You can't always get what you want."

"Yeah." He shrugged. I don't think he even understood my sarcasm. Finally, after a long silence, he stood up. "Guess I'll go home. Look, Suzy, is it OK if I call you sometime?"

"If you want to, well, it's all right," I said, feeling pressured by being asked in front of everyone.

"Yeah. Uh, I'll see you in English class Monday." He waved limply, then turned away.

Ellen and Donna both walked over to see if I wanted to talk. Of course I did.

"What did he want?" Ellen asked.

I shook my head as I explained, "I don't think Barry knows what he's doing right now. He's not going out with Peggy anymore—which is why I think he came to talk with me."

Donna asked softly, "Would you go out with him after everything that's happened?"

"I really don't know." I hoped I didn't sound as angry as I felt. "Barry didn't treat me very nicely. I'm surprised he's paying any attention to me again."

"What will you say if he asks you out?" Ellen whispered, casting a quick glance around at the party. It was silly, but we felt everyone must know what we were gossiping about. Everyone knew that Barry and I hadn't been seeing or really talking to one another.

"I don't know, I can't think about it now," I said sincerely. "Sometimes I think the only thing I want is for all the men in the world to be shipped to another planet!"

"Barry certainly played a big game with you, Suzy," Donna said honestly. "I guess you'll have to see what happens."

All that weekend I felt moody and bad-tempered. The only people I talked to were Donna—who told me she and Russ decided to see each other exclusively—and Jeff, who phoned to find out what time he should pick me up to go bowling.

I was so out of sorts that I couldn't really get into my date with Jeff. Trying to act enthusiastic that night was such a chore for me that after I carelessly steered my bowling ball into the gutter for the fourth time, I told l him I had an upset stomach and wanted to go home.

As Jeff was driving me home, I wondered if dating around was the right thing to do. Maybe it would have been better to stay with Mike. All I knew was that I wasn't happy this way. Yet I didn't know how to change.

I couldn't shake off my irritability, and even Patty made a point of staying out of my way for the rest of the weekend. The single thing that made me happy was that it was Thanksgiving week. We would have four days off, and my family was spending the whole vacation at Grandmom and Grandpop Powers's cabin in the Poconos. That meant that, for that weekend at least, I wouldn't have to worry about having dates—or not having a good time when I had them.

Chapter Ten

"The weekend in the Poconos was great. My grandpop walks at least two miles a day. He took Patty and me out for a short hike."

"You, hiking! I can't believe it," Donna teased.

I pushed her playfully on the arm. "Yes, me. You never realized how athletic I am."

"Well, I spent part of my weekend athletically—watching Russ's basketball game."

"Did we win?" I asked.

"Yeah, and you missed the victory party afterward."

"The party after the play was enough for me," I replied.

"Speaking of which," said Donna, "did Barry ever call you?"

"No. He said hello in school, but we haven't had any big conversations."

Donna said gently, "You know, Mike Kelly's been really bummed out the past couple of weeks—Russ told me."

"So what?" I said, wishing Donna wouldn't talk about Mike.

No matter how much I tried not to, I'd been thinking about him night and day. Each time I saw him in school, my heart fluttered wildly, and my palms got sweaty. I was learning one thing, and that was that it was impossible to to be just friends with a boy after you'd fallen for him. I kept telling myself I didn't know Mike well enough, or long enough, to be really in love. And that I didn't regret returning his ring. But that didn't make me feel any less miserable whenever I saw him.

"Hey, Suzy, it's me, Donna." She looked at me affectionately. "I know it's been rough for you, but you must feel something about Mike. Don't you miss him?"

I felt tears come to my eyes. I did miss Mike—a lot. And now with Barry coming around, it was all too confusing. I resorted to what had become my usual defense. "I won't go out with only one guy, Donna. And Mike won't see me unless I do."

I thought a look of pity crossed Donna's face. "Well, it's not so bad having a steady boyfriend, honestly. I'm glad I'm going out with Russ." She said gently, "Think about it, Suze."

Donna turned to the stereo and started to look for an album to play. We didn't talk about it anymore.

Everything seemed to be going wrong at that point. My hospital work had become difficult ever since Mrs. Jaworski's condition had gotten worse. Some days when I'd stop by her room, she was in too much pain to chat.

I didn't realize how torn up inside I was until one afternoon when I returned home from the hospital. After a simple question from my mother about dinner that night, I burst into tears.

"What is it, Suzy?" My mother looked at me closely. "Tell me, darling."

"It's poor Mrs. Jaworski," I sobbed, and my mother took me in her arms. "Oh, Mom, she's so sweet and so full of life, and now she's going to die! It's not fair!"

My mother squeezed me tightly, then said,

"Come into the kitchen, and we'll have a cup of tea and talk about it." She led me out of the living room.

"It sounds as if she's had a full, wonderful life, Suzy," she remarked after I'd told her all about Mrs. Jaworski. "People who reach her age and whose lives have been worthwhile can accept death without qualms. She's very old and unwell. I'm sure she'd choose to go peacefully rather than live on and on in pain."

"But how can I be a doctor when seeing people suffer upsets me so much? Doctors must be terribly cold people."

"I don't think that's true," my mother said thoughtfully, taking a sip of her spiced tea. "All the doctors I've ever known are human beings like the rest of us. But they've accepted the inevitability of death, and though they do all they can to help people, they realize that no one's life can go on forever. We all grow old and die someday, Suzy. Nobody in the whole world can change that."

"But why?" I persisted, knowing I was asking the unanswerable. "Why does everything have to end in some way or another?"

"Because something ends doesn't mean it isn't worthwhile. Every time I discover a new gray hair, I know I'm getting older. Every day that I live shortens my life. But does that mean I shouldn't be happy to be alive, that I shouldn't savor every moment? Time can't stand still. If it did, there'd be nothing to live for."

"Don't talk like that, Mom," I begged, crying anew. "I can't bear to think that you won't always be here."

My mother looked at me and sighed. "And sometimes I can't bear to think that soon you'll be leaving to go away to school, then marry and have your career and family. But it's going to happen, no matter how I feel about it. I'd have been a pretty silly woman not to have had children just because I couldn't stand the thought of their growing up one day."

"Why does it have to hurt so much to love people, Mom? If caring about people means either feeling sad or being hurt, I'd rather not care at all!" I shook my head angrily.

"But caring's what life's all about, Suzy. You have to accept the pain to receive the joy," my mother gently persisted.

It seemed too cruel and complicated to me. I tried to trust what my mother had said, but it gave me little comfort. I lay in bed that night thinking, *Maybe I'll never get married at all. If caring about people means getting hurt, I'd rather be alone forever.*

The next morning, my mood was no brighter. I sat sulkily over my oatmeal and juice as I ran over everything in my mind. I didn't understand anything anymore. The fun-filled life that I was trying to live was turning out to be a dismal failure. I couldn't go out on first dates with every boy in the junior class, nor did I want to. But what was the alternative? Going out with somebody only to wait for the day when it suddenly ended?

Nobody else seemed to be having the same problems. Donna had settled down peacefully with Russ. His athletic fervor no longer bothered her as long as they were together. She was busy after school, anyway, doing odd jobs and writing stories for the newspaper.

Ginny and Peter spent almost all their time together now. She was blossoming, and she and Peter were thinking of collaborating on their own play.

Ellen had adjusted, too, even though she was not going out with Denny. She was dating and looking for a steady boyfriend. "But as long as I leave myself open to meeting new people," she told me, "there's always a chance that the next guy will be the one." Her explanation echoed in my mind.

Now, as I sat toying with my breakfast, Patty interrupted my thoughts. "Earth to Suzy, Earth to Suzy. Come in!" She waved her hand in front of my face.

"Very funny, Patty."

"What are you thinking about? Boys again?"

"No, if you really want to know, I was thinking about my biology club presentation this afternoon."

Patty looked at me and smirked. "Sure, sure."

I was glad when my mother stepped in. "Patty, I think you've said enough. Finish your breakfast—I want to get you to school on time."

But that dreary breakfast set my mood for the rest of the day. I just couldn't shake my blues. I dragged through classes, and even my presentation at the bio club didn't cheer me up. I didn't get out of school until it was already dark outside. There's something really depressing about missing a whole day of sunlight. I was just leaving the building to head home when Barry met me at the door.

"Hi, Suzy, had a late meeting?"

"Oh, hi, Barry, yes, we just finished with

the bio club. What are you doing around so late?"

He looked away and then into my eyes. I noticed how blue they were. We hadn't been so near one another since that night in the diner.

"Well, to be honest, I was waiting for you. Can I give you a ride home?" I knew this was special because Barry had to borrow his brother's car.

I looked at him, hesitating, and then he grabbed my hand. "I won't bite." He smiled. Barry could sure be sweet when he wanted. We walked to the car.

"How have you been, Barry?" I asked as he held the car door open for me.

"Fine, fine," he said casually. Then he paused and turned to me before he started the car. "I've got these tickets to the Black Orchid concert Friday. Want to go with me?"

"I don't know, Barry," I said slowly. It was too much for me to be in his car again, to be so close again after all this time.

He started the car, and drove out of the parking lot. I waited to hear what he would say.

"I know I hurt you, Suzy. I'm sorry." He

124

paused. "Peggy was a mistake. You're the only girl for me."

Old feelings swept over me. Could he really mean it? "I wish I could believe you, Barry. I—"

He interrupted me. "Give me another chance." Then he took my hand gently. "Suzy, you know we belong together. Please come with me on Friday night."

I was so tired of all the thoughts going on in my head that I gave in. "OK, Barry. Friday night."

"Great," he said.

We decided on a time, and Barry said he'd be able to get his brother's car that night. By that time we were at my house. I quickly jumped out of his car. "See you," I called as I ran up the path. But I felt sort of relieved when he pulled the car out of the driveway.

Chapter Eleven

Over the next couple of days, I tried to figure out what it was going to be like to be with Barry again. I imagined different scenarios depending on my mood: I'd be anxious and ill at ease; I'd fall in love with him all over again right from the start; I'd seethe with resentment and lash out at him for what he'd done to me. But I resigned myself to the fact that I was taking a big chance. And the night of the date, I couldn't resist the same feeling of anticipation I had before my very first date with Barry.

By the time I'd chosen an outfit, half the clothes in my closet were draped around the room. I chose a pair of designer jeans with my new boots and a pale blue puff-sleeved angora sweater.

Then I ran downstairs to eat quickly before showering and washing my hair. I must have really been shoveling in my barbecued chicken and scalloped potatoes because Dad laughed and said, "Whoa, Suzy! You'd better come up for air soon, or you'll have a stomachache before the night's out."

Patty snorted. "Brother! It's like you and Barry never broke up, you know? First time he asks you out again, you totally lose your cool."

"When I want your advice, twerp, I'll ask for it," I said with as much dignity as I could manage, considering the barbecue sauce smeared all over my face. I turned to Mom. "May I be excused now, please?"

"No dessert? I baked an apricot crumb pie this afternoon."

"I'll take her piece." Leave it to Patty never to miss an opening.

"Oh, no, you won't," I said. "I'll have it when I come home, Mom. As for you"—I rose from the table and gave Patty what I considered a crushing look—"I've heard you talking about Ricky Reese. You've got a full-fledged adolescent crush on him." That shut her up pretty quickly.

I strode from the room, but I bumped my hip on the doorjamb, which kind of messed up my regal act.

Then, too soon, it was quarter to eight. Barry would be here any minute, I thought. I took a good, long look at myself in the full-length mirror attached to my closet door.

"Not bad if I do say so myself," I murmured, taking in everything, from the smoky blue eyeshadow and smudge of gray crayon that widened my eyes, to the blue and green feathered barrette that pulled my hair back on the right side.

I'm ready for this date, I thought.

Barry arrived, and I strode downstairs with the poise of a movie star. It was all an act, though, because inside I was terrified.

"Hi, Suzy, you look terrific," Barry said.

"Thanks, Barry." I felt awkward. "I'll get my jacket so we can get going."

My mother waved goodbye happily, calling out, as usual, "Have a good time."

Barry looked gorgeous. But after everything that had happened between us, he now acted as if we'd never stopped dating. He kept up a steady stream of chatter over the Fleetwood Mac tape playing on the tape deck.

"I had to pay Marv twenty bucks to use his wheels tonight, but that's no big deal for me," he bragged. "I made a lot of money this summer. Big tips from all those housewives who thought I was cute when I carried their groceries to their cars for them. And I've still got plenty. Of course, the tape's mine. Marv's taste in music is terrible."

I hardly knew how to answer. I was bored and very disappointed. Never once during the ride did he ask anything about me. Why hadn't I ever noticed that almost every word that came out of his mouth was about himself? After being separated for so long, you'd have thought Barry and I would have had more to talk about than his brother's car and his own new shoes. But every time I made an attempt to turn the conversation to something that didn't personally involve Barry, he'd switch it. I was glad when we reached the auditorium. At the concert we wouldn't have much of a chance to talk.

There were a lot of people waiting in line to get in. Once we were inside, we made our way to our seats, which were in the middle of the hall. I loved the excitement before a concert. I could tell everyone was psyched about Black Orchid. There was a buzz of conversation, an incredible feeling of electricity in the air.

When the houselights went down and the first band started playing, some of the seats were still vacant. There were two different groups, so I figured some peopele would arrive after the opening band, which usually was not as good as the headliner.

Black Orchid finally came on and whipped the audience into a frenzy. They opened with a few fast numbers, then did a slow, romantic song (I thought about Mike all the way through it), and then did a few more loud ones. By the end we were all on our feet, clapping along, singing the choruses, dancing.

All too soon, the lights came on. We clapped and clapped, but the band wouldn't come on again. Everyone lit matches and held them above their heads until the whole stadium glowed. Finally people began to leave.

Barry tugged at my arm. "C'mon, Suzy, or we'll never get out of here," he said impatiently.

Suddenly, as I stood up and put on my jacket, I saw Mike. I might have been standing in the middle of a desert island as I watched him. He led a girl through the surging, rowdy crowd, her hand firmly held in his. This night had been too much of a shock. First, finding out the truth about how self-centered Barry was, then seeing Mike with another girl.

I wanted to cry, to call after Mike and stop him. Instead, I got to my feet like a zombie and followed Barry down the row and up the aisle. I might have been sleepwalking for all the awareness I had of my surroundings.

"What'll it be?" Barry asked when we got to the car. He was still too caught up in himself to notice how quiet and uncommunicative I'd become. "The diner?"

"No, not the diner!" I blurted out, unable to face the possibility that Mike would be there with his date. I tried to push the desperation from my face and my voice. "I'm too hungry to wait that long to eat," I fibbed. "Let's go to that pizza place down the road from here."

"Aw, that joint's always quiet as a tomb," he protested.

The only way to get through to Barry was to be firm. "Barry, I want to have pizza, OK?"

He gave me a surprised look, then murmured, "OK."

On the way to the pizza place, Barry talked

about the concert. "Black Orchid was great, but the set was too short. Just because we're a small town doesn't mean it had to be short," he complained.

"I know what you mean, the tickets—"

"Were too expensive for that little time," he cut me off rudely.

I tried to think of something that he'd listen to. "The first band wasn't bad, but I think the sound system was too loud. What do you think?"

"They were OK, but it wasn't the sound system. They needed more practice—they didn't know how to jam. You know what that is?"

I said, "Yes, I do." But Barry didn't hear me.

"It's when they start playing from the original piece of music and go off into their own creation. It's also called improvisation."

We got to the pizza parlor, and as I expected, I enjoyed the pizza more than I enjoyed Barry's conversation. The whole evening, Barry might as well have been boring old Jack Carlton instead of the boy I'd been crazy about.

"You've gotten awfully quiet all of a sudden," he said after a stretch of silence.

I almost laughed out loud at that. Barry

had been so busy telling me what he thought of each and every member of the band that I was astounded he even noticed I hadn't said much. He'd been doing a monologue, so what was wrong with having an audience?

But there was no way to tell him this, so I simply said, "The first band was too loud. Too much music in one night for me."

He accepted my explanation, maybe because he just didn't care.

"You want to stop at the diner real quick just for a soda?" he asked as we pulled on our jackets to leave.

I shook my head. "Not tonight. I'm really done in," I insisted. "Why don't you go there after you drop me off?"

"Maybe I will," he answered shortly, a stubborn look making his usually cute face mulish. That expression was familiar, but I'd forgotten about it since the summer, just as I'd forgotten how sullen he got when he wasn't given his own way.

We finally arrived at my house. I was expecting a kiss—Barry wouldn't leave me without it. But I knew it could never be the same as the kisses that used to melt me. Barry hugged me, in the same old familiar way, but I didn't respond at all. I just felt tense.

Abruptly he let go of me. 'What's the matter with you, Suzy?" He sounded more annoyed than worried.

He didn't understand that it was over. Tears came to my eyes, and I looked away for a moment. I hated having to say this. "We can't go out together—it won't work, Barry," I said gently.

"I know—it's Peggy," he angrily announced. Then his voice softened. "Look, Suzy—I told you, she was a mistake."

I wished I could say yes to Barry, but I couldn't. His behavior that night still sent an angry twinge through me. "I know, Barry, I still can't," I persisted.

"But, Suzy, you're the best," he said as he caressed my hands. "We belong together. Please try, Suzy."

I could hear the loneliness in his voice. I realized that I didn't bear a grudge against him anymore. And I didn't want to hurt him or get back at him as I'd thought I would.

"Whatever we had together is gone," I said firmly. "I'm still your friend. But," I added, shaking my head, "I don't want to be anything more."

I started to get out of the car, but his hand on my shoulder stopped me. "Suzy, wait," he pleaded. "Try to remember what a great couple we used to be."

"I'm sorry, Barry. It just won't work."

With that, I got out of the car, closed it gently behind me, and made my way up the path and into the darkened house.

I didn't bother cutting myself a piece of Mom's pie before I went upstairs. How could I eat anything with the churning going on in my stomach? I poured a glass of milk and took it up to my room with me, hoping it would calm me. I felt agitated; I knew it wasn't going to be easy to fall asleep.

As I changed into my nightgown, I thought about the evening. Seeing Barry had made everything clear. I didn't feel hatred toward him for what he'd done to me. He was as mixed up and unsure of himself as I was. I suddenly realized I had been so busy making sure no one would ever hurt me again that I hadn't let myself feel the true pain of our breakup. If I hadn't pretended that I didn't care, I wouldn't have hurled myself into a round of meaningless dating.

Seeing Barry had acted like a big eraser on a murky blackboard. Suddenly all my illusions and self-deception had been wiped away. For the first time since that fateful summer morning, I was free to look at things I'd hidden from myself all this time.

I'd known I didn't want to get hurt again, but I hadn't realized what that meant. In my fear I'd become closed and selfish. I'd refused to allow myself to care for people, to give to them, and that meant that I couldn't receive from them, either. I realized now how alone I was and how lonely I'd continue to be if I didn't open up, didn't take the chance of loving someone.

Was it too late, I wondered, to convince Mike I was willing to take the risk? Mom was right. It was better to have *something* and take the chance of being hurt than to have nothing at all. Feeling nothing at all was the same as being dead inside. Ever since Barry had told me he loved someone else, I'd wasted most of my energy trying to kill my true emotions. I'd tried to protect myself from anything that might hurt me, only to discover that I had nothing. And having nothing hurt more than anything in the whole world.

Seeing Mike with someone else had hurt, too. It was something I'd never let myself think about, fooling myself into believing that Mike would rather be alone if he couldn't be with me.

I tossed and turned all night, but by morning I'd made up my mind to try to change my life. I'd be a fool if I told myself I didn't care this time, if I let Mike slip from my life. I'd driven Mike out of my life. Now it was up to me to get him back into it.

Chapter Twelve

Saturday was the best day I'd had in weeks. Part of it was due to Donna's company—I hadn't seen her outside of school since right after my trip to the Poconos. Part of it was because of the beautiful, clear, crisp day and the fun we had ice-skating. But most of it was that I hadn't felt so sure of myself since Barry had broken up with me. For the first time since the summer, I wasn't hurt and confused.

I came bursting into the kitchen at the end of the day with so much energy that my skates fell off my shoulders.

My mother laughed. "Well, you had a good

time, didn't you?" she said, picking up the skates. I shrugged out of my coat and gloves.

"Oh, it was great, Mom." I sat down at the table.

"I'll make you some hot chocolate."

"Terrific. I need something hot to drink." I paused. "And, Mom, I wanted to tell you. You were right as usual."

My mother smiled. "About what?"

"It *is* better to care about people. At the same time that I was protecting myself from hurt, I was denying myself love. I haven't been open to very much besides my own problems."

"I'm glad to hear you say that," my mother said gently. "I know you've been scared. We all are sometimes in our lives."

"I think, Mom, that I really like this guy, but I chased him away. I'm going to try to talk to him again."

"Good for you, Suzy." Mom took my hand and squeezed it supportively.

Patty came storming in at that moment with her friend Laurie.

"Can we have some hot chocolate?"

"Of course, Patty. I just have to finish discussing something with your sister." I looked

139

at Patty and playfully stuck my tongue out at her.

"That's OK, Mom. I know what to do now," I said.

I felt cheerful all evening. Finally, I was putting some sense back into my life.

I'd been avoiding Mike at school ever since our talk. My new mission was to go out of my way to run into him and always give him a big hello when I did. He always had a warm smile and a cheerful "Hi, Suze" when we passed in the halls. But we never exchanged more than a few sentences.

Then, during one of our conversations—in the cafeteria line—he mentioned that he was working at Bennington's again on Monday and Thursday nights during the preholiday rush. That stuck in my mind, and on the way home from the hospital Thursday I decided to stop at Bennington's.

At first I didn't see Mike. I was so nervous I almost left, but I made myself stay instead, spinning the rack of ties in one corner while I looked for him.

Then I saw him coming out of a door that must have led to the back storerooms. He was wearing a gray flannel blazer over his white oxford shirt, as all the other Bennington clerks did (even the saleswomen wore white blouses and gray jackets). He looked so cute I could almost feel my heart expand in my chest. I finally knew how truly special a person he was, and I wanted, more than anything, to tell him so.

My eyes must have been burning holes in his back as he assisted a well-dressed, white-haired man in choosing a shirt, because as soon as the man took his purchase to the cashier, Mike turned and looked straight at me.

I smiled—it was more a frightened little twitch of the lips than a real smile, but he came right over.

"Hello, Suzy," he said amiably. "What brings you here?"

"Just looking for a Christmas present for my dad." That was only half a lie, I told myself. I really did need something for Dad.

"Have you seen the new ties we just got in? I think your dad would look great in one."

All I could do was murmur no, that I hadn't seen them, and follow Mike as he led me to a counter display.

"The green and blue combination's nice," Mike pointed out. "Or maybe the brown and tan is more your father's style. He's a pretty conservative dresser."

"Yes, the brown and tan," I said. "I'll take that."

I followed Mike back to the counter where he'd left his salesbook. I had to say something, and soon, I thought feverishly, while he was writing up the order. Otherwise, I'd be on my way to the cashier and out of the store in a second. None of this was going the way I'd envisioned it.

"You know, we—we really haven't had a chance to talk in a long time," I said uncertainly.

"No, we haven't." Mike tore the check from the book and handed it to me along with the tie. "We'll have to do that one of these days."

Clutching the tie, I took a deep breath and asked, my voice unnaturally high-pitched, "How about Saturday night? You could come by the house after dinner." Now that I'd started, I couldn't stop. My words came out in a rush. "Mom and Dad are going to a party, and there's a good movie on cable at nine o'clock. I can't remember what it is, but I know it's something worth seeing."

A flicker of something that looked like pleasure touched his face. Then it disappeared, seriousness replacing it.

"I'm sorry, Suzy, but I'm afraid I can't."

I smiled, trying to conceal the devastating effect of his rejection. "I hope I wasn't being too pushy," I said brightly. "I mean, you're not going with somebody or anything, are you?"

He smiled at that, and I thought he looked a little sad. "No, it's not that. It's just—"

"Excuse me, young man. Can you help me find the proper size sweater, please?" A middle-aged woman came up next to me. "It's for my son, and he's just about your size."

Mike's genial, professional smile came back on. "Certainly. I'll be happy to help," he told her with a willingness that would have melted any mother's heart. "Lead the way to the sweaters you have in mind."

She was already crossing the store as he came out from behind the counter. "Look, Suzy, I'm sorry I can't talk. Sorry I can't come Saturday night, either. But I don't think it's a good idea."

I smiled so brightly he might have been telling an amusing story instead of asking me, in so many words, to stay out of his life. "Sure, Mike. No problem."

143

Well, that's that, I told myself philosophically as I plodded home in the gathering dusk. I walked carefully, avoiding the patches of ice on the sidewalks. Nothing ventured, nothing gained. At least I'd given it my best shot. If Mike didn't want anything to do with me, I couldn't blame him. I couldn't do anything about it, either.

"Is that you, Suzy?" Mom called from the back of the house as the front door slammed shut behind me.

"Uh-huh," I called, hanging my jacket in the hall and dropping my package on the hall table. Then I made my way to the kitchen.

Mom was slicing Bermuda onions and radishes for salad when I dumped my books on the kitchen table. "Patty's having dinner at her friend Emmy's house, and your dad's got a late meeting, so it'll be just the two of us for dinner," she said without looking up. "I thought we'd take potluck—cold leftover beef and salad—in front of the TV."

"That's fine," I mumbled.

She set down her knife. "Now, let's see. All we have to do is to wash the greens." She sniffled. "Darn those onions!"

Maybe it was the sight of the tears running down Mom's cheeks from the onion slicing, or maybe it was that I couldn't keep my misery bottled up another minute. I took one look at her, and tears started pouring down my cheeks.

"Suzy, what is it?" she asked, wiping her hands on the apron tied around her middle. She sat down on the chair next to mine. "It's not Mrs. Jaworski again, is it?"

"No, no," I said through my tears, which were turning into a waterworks. "It's me. Oh, Mom, I'm so miserable I could die! I ruined everything with Mike! Now he doesn't want to have anything to do with me. I was so sure he still cared, but he doesn't. He doesn't care at all!"

"There, there." She patted my back. "Let me get a tissue so you can dry your eyes. Then why don't you tell me all about it? It might make you feel better, you know."

"Better!" My voice cracked as a fresh flood of tears poured down my cheeks. "I'll never feel better! I've wrecked my whole life."

My mother was terrific. She sat stroking my hair and patting my shoulder until my sobs dwindled down to little hiccups.

"Now," she said, when I was finally calmed down enough to blow my nose, "start at the beginning and tell me what's been getting you down. I noticed you've been upset, but I thought it was Barry you cared about, not Mike."

That started my tears all over again, though it was more of a trickle this time since I was pretty much all cried out.

"Oh, Mom, I've been such an idiot!" I said when I could finally speak. "I've tried to straighten everything out, but it's too late."

Once I started talking, I couldn't stop. I must have talked for an hour.

Mom listened earnestly, one elbow propped on the kitchen table and her chin resting on her palm. She didn't interrupt or try to stop me, and I just kept talking, letting out everything I'd been keeping to myself—and *from* myself—for so long.

"So you see," I finished, "it's just no use. I've botched up everything, and now I know it's Mike I've wanted all along, but he doesn't want me anymore."

"I think you may be wrong," she said. "But let's get out of this kitchen and have something to eat. If you'll get the TV tables set up, I'll wash the lettuce. Then you can toss the salad things together while I slice some meat. And then," she said, winking, "we'll see if your old mom can't give you some advice while we have a bite to eat."

Advice is exactly what she did give me, with a dash of sympathy and a pinch of reality thrown in. "What you've been through is awful, darling," she said when we were finally seated side by side on the sofa, our plates on trays in front of us. "And I don't think you should keep blaming yourself. You haven't done anything so awful, you know, and you didn't do anything so unfathomable, either. Anyone can understand another person being hurt and afraid of being hurt again.

"And I'm proud that you've found it in your heart to forgive and understand Barry. I can still remember being a teenager, Suzy, and I know it's not easy. But," she added softly, "I still think you've been lying to yourself."

"Lying to myself! But, Mom, I've never leveled with myself like this before. I've finally sifted through all my feelings about Barry and Mike. I'm being perfectly honest."

"Are you, dear?" she asked mildly. "I don't think you've been as honest with Mike as you could have been—or with yourself, for that matter. You say you put yourself on the line with Mike today, but did you? Did you tell him how you feel or why you acted the way you did or how much you'd like to see him again? That's taking a risk, Suzy. And that's the only way you'll have a chance of convincing him you're not the same frivolous girl you seemed to be."

"You mean, tell Mike he's the only guy I care about? Mom, I couldn't do that! What if he told me he couldn't care less? I'd be humiliated!"

"At least you'd know what Mike really feels. This way, you know nothing. You don't even know why he turned down your invitation, do you?"

"No. I figured it was because he never wants to see me again."

"Haven't you considered that nobody likes getting hurt? And from what you've told me, you've hurt Mike once. Maybe he's shying away from you because he doesn't want to risk getting hurt by you again."

"You think so? But then why didn't he tell me that when I saw him?"

Mom laughed softly. "Suzy, Suzy, don't you see? You're not willing to confess *your* feelings to Mike, but you expect him to be totally frank with you. Is that fair?"

"Maybe you're right," I admitted. "But I'm

afraid I'll shatter into a trillion pieces if he tells me he doesn't like me anymore."

"That's the chance you'll have to take, I'm afraid. But you've got to give him a chance, too, honey. Boys aren't so different from girls. They feel happy and sad and brave and scared just as we do. Now, let's have some rocky road ice cream and see what's on TV, and then you can help me look for my sewing glasses so I can work on my needlepoint."

And as I was eating my ice cream, I decided that Mom had given me some great advice. But I wasn't ready for it yet. I wasn't willing to face another rejection from Mike. *I'll just give myself a few days to think it over*, I thought. *Maybe Mike will approach me.*

No such luck. The next day in school, Mike gave me a friendly greeting as usual, but no more than that. I came home from school dragging my feet, not looking forward to the weekend that lay ahead of me. I'd turned down three dates and had nothing planned. I needed the time to do some serious thinking.

Mom was sitting behind a row of flower-pots she'd lined up on the dining room table when I came in. She was busily pinching back and pruning some of her houseplants.

She looked over with an expectant expression on her face as I came in.

"How did it go with Mike today?" she asked.

"I couldn't do it, Mom," I confessed, feeling more cowardly than ever. "I need the weekend to think things over."

She nodded. "That's always a good idea, Suzy. No reason to rush into this and speak before you think."

"I'll try to talk to him Monday."

"What have you got planned for tonight?"

I shrugged. "Nothing. All my girlfriends have dates, and right now I'm not wild about the idea of going out with anyone." *With anyone but Mike*, I added to myself, knowing my mother was probably saying the same thing to herself.

"Good!" Leave it to Mom to look at the bright side. "Then you can go with Patty and your dad and me to the mall. They're lighting the big Christmas tree tonight, and the carolers are going to sing."

I almost told her I'd rather stay home. Then I changed my mind. I couldn't think twenty-four hours a day, and there was no reason to make myself more miserable.

As it turned out, I had a wonderful time. I'd been so preoccupied with my own soap opera lately, I hadn't given much thought to how much I enjoyed being with my family. After the tree-lighting ceremony, we stopped for sundaes, then sang Christmas carols ourselves all the way home.

The next day I took the bus to the center of town to do Christmas shopping, and meet Donna for lunch at Mona's.

I hadn't planned to bare my soul to anyone but Mom, but as Donna and I sat eating our soup and sandwiches in the warm and cozy back dining room of Mona's, I found myself telling her the gist of my problem as well as my mother's advice on the subject.

"Gee, and here I thought you'd end up getting back together with Barry," Donna exclaimed. "It goes to show that you never know what's on somebody's mind till they tell you, doesn't it?"

I took a spoonful of soup and started on my egg salad sandwich. "What do you think I should do, Donna?"

"Take your mom's advice," she said simply. "Look, Suzy, if I hadn't plunged in and told Russ how much it bothered me that he was so committed to all those sports, do you think we'd be going together today? You can't always keep things to yourself."

"But what if he still doesn't want to see me?" I asked fretfully. "What if I do it all for nothing?"

"It doesn't sound as if you'd be any more upset than you are now. And at least Mike will know you're not just a shallow flirt. At least he'll respect you, Suzy."

"That's a good point," I agreed, wondering why it hadn't occurred to me. After all, I hadn't given Mike many reasons to think I was less superficial than I'd acted, had I?

"But if he doesn't care—" I broke off and shuddered. "I can't go back to dating a lot of guys again, Donna."

"Well, you don't have to go out with every guy who asks you, you know," she reminded me. "You can be popular without having a date every night."

"I know, I know. And I've certainly accomplished more now that I've jumped off that crazy merry-go-round I was on. That's settled then," I said with more assurance than I felt. "I'll talk to Mike on Monday."

"You'll feel a lot better if you do," Donna encouraged me. "Look at it this way: you've got nothing to lose."

But I did. I had my pride. And if Mike took that away from me, I didn't think I'd ever be able to face him again.

Chapter Thirteen

That's what I found myself thinking as I hung out by the door Monday after classes, pretending I was reading the notices on the bulletin board when I was really waiting for Mike. Every minute dragged by like an hour. A couple of kids looked at me curiously as they said goodbye, no doubt wondering who I was waiting for. If I hadn't seen Mike's car on the far side of the asphalt lot, I'd have been worried I'd missed him. Now I just worried that he was staying late for some awful reason. Or maybe he was waiting for someone, too, some girl.

Finally, I saw him about thirty feet down

the hall, heading toward me. I wheeled back to the notice board, then slowly turned around again. I'd said I was going to be totally frank this time around. That meant there was no reason to pretend I was doing anything other than waiting to talk to him.

"See you tomorrow," he said, smiling as he started to pass by.

"Please . . . wait, Mike." I didn't exactly block his way, but I didn't want him to leave before I had a chance to talk to him.

He stopped and came over to me. "You mean you've been waiting for *me*?" he asked. "Sorry. I didn't mean to walk right by you. I figured you were meeting somebody else."

"There are some things I have to say to you," I began. Then, afraid that might sound as if I were looking for a fight, I added, "Things that mean a lot to me. Do you think we could talk a few minutes?"

"Um, sure. Uh, I don't know why not." He stumbled over the words. "But I've got to be at work in fifteen minutes. . . ."

"If you don't mind, I can drive over with you and walk from there." I was unwilling to let this chance escape me. If I didn't explain myself to Mike this time, I was afraid I'd never get up the nerve again.

"That's fine," he told me, but he sounded hesitant.

"You sound as if hearing what's on my mind is a fate worse than death," I said as we walked across the lot. I didn't want to be flippant, but at the same time, I wanted Mike to know I wasn't about to start either accusing him of anything or throwing myself at him.

He smiled as he unlocked the car. "It's not that," he said. "I guess I'm a little worried that you're angry at me because I turned down your invitation for Saturday night."

That was my opening, and I took it. "I'm not mad at all, Mike." I slid into the front seat. "As a matter of fact, I don't blame you in the least for not wanting to see me again."

He gave me a questioning look, but I didn't speak, so he started the ignition. We were both silent as we drove toward Bennington's, I because I was overwhelmed by emotion at being back in Mike's car sitting next to him, Mike because he was probably completely confused by my behavior.

We'd driven a minute or two in silence when I finally continued. "You see, I realize I haven't behaved like the kind of girl you'd ever want to go out with again. But I *do* want to see you

155

again, Mike, and I figure I owe you an explanation. None of the things I said to you about not wanting to have a steady relationship were true." He looked at me in surprise, and I quickly went on, "I didn't realize that at the time, though. I thought I meant each and every word. I was fooling myself into believing the way to have fun was to date every guy around. I fooled myself into thinking that I really was having fun. Now I see it's just because I was afraid of getting hurt again, the way Barry hurt me. But all the time I'd rather have been with you, Mike. I'd give anything if we could start all over again."

We'd pulled into the lot behind Bennington's. Mike shut off the engine, then leaned his head back against the seat, closing his eyes. "It's too late to start all over again, Suzy."

"Why, Mike?" I persisted. "If it's that you've found another girl you like better than me, I can understand. Or if you've decided I'm a horrible person and can't stand me, just say so." I stopped talking and sat waiting for him to say the words that would destroy me. Then Mike opened his eyes and looked at me tenderly.

"Of course I don't think you're horrible, Suzy," he said softly, reaching out. He almost took one of my hands in his, then thought better of it and pulled back quickly. "And there's nobody else, either."

"I saw you at the rock concert," I confessed. "You were with a girl."

"She was no one special, just a date," he said. "Did you expect me to go into a monastery because you didn't want my ring? I'll admit I felt like it a few times, but I finally decided I was an idiot if I sat home all the time while you were obviously having so much fun."

"But I wasn't, Mike!" I insisted. "I wasn't having fun at all."

He smiled, and this time he did reach over and take my hand. I returned the pressure gently.

"I believe you, Suzy, especially since I almost did the same thing."

"You did?"

"I was knocked off my feet when you gave my ring back. I couldn't accept what you'd said, and all I could think was that I cared enough to make a commitment and you didn't. So at first I told myself it didn't matter, that I wouldn't have been happy with you, anyway. But I finally realized that I *did* feel bad. After that, I realized I'd better stop pretending and start trying to be my old self again. But at first I was tempted to go out with any girl who'd take me and to flaunt it in your face so you'd see I didn't care. I suppose that's the way you felt about Barry."

"And now?" I whispered.

"Now I don't know how involved I want to get again," he answered. "How do I know you won't wake up one day and decide you still really like Barry Howell?"

"You don't have to worry about that," I assured him fervently. "I was with Barry that night I saw you at the concert. Since he was my first real boyfriend, I guess I saw him in a special light both before and after we broke up. Being with him again made me realize that Barry's Mr. Cool act gets in the way of being the nice person he could be." I grimaced, remembering that dreary evening. "Barry and I did like each other once. But that's over."

"You really don't care about dating other guys anymore?" he asked, his brow knit in doubt. "You wouldn't feel you were missing out on lots of things, on excitement, if you were with me?"

"Mike, I can't think of anything more exciting than being with you," I said. "Please forgive me and give me another chance!"

He didn't say anything at first. He sat staring out the windshield, which was already starting to sparkle with frost. I didn't rush him. I'd said what I had to say, and now all I could do was let him mull it over. Even though I was quaking inside, afraid he'd say "Forget it," I felt as if an enormous burden had been lifted off my shoulders.

"I want to, Suzy," he said at last. "I can't tell you how much I want to. But—"

A sharp breath caught in my throat.

"But we'll have to go slowly this time," he said. I went limp with relief. "Maybe I was at fault, too. Maybe I rushed things. And maybe if I'd ever been willing to mention Barry, we might have talked things out and gotten things straight. But we did make a mess of things, and I don't want either of us to get hurt all over again. So, we'll take it nice and easy, all right?"

"OK," I agreed, feeling even happier when he leaned over and kissed me. It was a light kiss, but it was magical.

"Now I'd better race inside and get behind the counter, or I'll be amongst the ranks of the unemployed," Mike said and laughed, sounding more like his old self again. "And keep this Friday night free for me," he added, as we hopped out of the car and he headed toward the back door of the store.

The temperature had dropped since this morning, and there was a promise of snow in the air, but I felt warm and snug in spite of the wind and cold. Mike was giving me another chance, and that made me feel warmer inside than sitting in front of an open fire.

Epilogue

It's been almost a year now since Mike and I had that talk in Bennington's parking lot. Mike just never got around to offering me his ring again. But not because things haven't worked out. I guess we both knew I didn't need his ring to show how much I cared for him. Trusting someone means a lot more than having someone's ring hanging around your neck.

He's in Philadelphia now, in his first year at Temple. We don't get to see each other as often as we did, but he comes home almost every weekend, and I've made a few day-trips there to see him. He promises he'll get home to take me to my senior prom.

Mike and I don't know what will happen in the next few years. We're both serious about our education, and everyone knows that studying to be a doctor isn't easy. Right now we like to fantasize about getting married someday and having a medical practice together, but if that day ever comes, it's a long way off.

In the meantime, we've got a wonderful, healthy relationship. I no longer worry about whether or not Mike's going to get tired of me someday and break up or whether our happiness will last forever. I've learned to take one day at a time and be thankful I've found a guy like Mike. But if I'm ever in the position of playing the field again, I'll know better than to play it with a vengeance.

Mrs. Jaworski passed away soon after the New Year. I was sad, and I know I'll never forget her. But losing one of my favorite patients didn't make me want to quit my work at the hospital the way I'd feared it might. There are still plenty of others whose days need brightening. How could I ever leave all the children who need me so much? Each time one gets well enough to go home, I feel proud of the doctors and nurses—and myself—because we made it possible.

Things change, of course, as Mom tried to tell me they did. Peter and Ginny are still together, and they're hoping to go to the American Academy of Dramatic Arts in New York City after graduation. Donna and Russ broke up over the summer, but they're back together again—for how long, not even Donna will venture to guess. As for Ellen, she never did find her Mr. Right junior year, but over the summer, working as a camp counselor at a local day camp, she met someone new. His name's Chad Goodwin, and he wants to be a phys. ed. instructor one day. He's a freshman at the junior college here, so Ellen's got her full-time boyfriend as last. Joanie Ellis is now going steady with Jack Carlton, maybe because she's the only one who'll laugh at his jokes.

There are only two other items of interest.

Barry Howell is a real ladies' man these days, dating lots of girls from his college as well as girls from other schools in the area. I think he loves his playboy image, and if that's what suits him, who am I to criticize?

And then there's my sister Patty. She's got a full-blown crush on a boy. But I've resisted the temptation to tease her when she mopes around the house, darting glances at the phone. How could I laugh at her? I know all too well how it feels!

Don't miss these great new *Sweet Dreams* romances, on sale soon!

☐ **#51 MAGIC MOMENTS by Debra Spector (On sale November 15, 1983 • 23757-8 • $1.95)**
—As an amateur magician, Nicki was delighted when Perry Ingram, one of the best young magicians in the state, walked into her life. But lately Perry has been appearing more frequently with Lana, his gorgeous assistant. Nicki's afraid that her magic isn't enough to keep Perry from breaking her heart—and disappearing forever.

☐ **#52 LOVE NOTES by Joanna Campbell (On sale November 15, 1983 • 23758-6 • $1.95)**
—There's nothing Kirsten wants more than to be a concert pianist—unless it's Peter, the violinist she's met at the Greenacres Summer Music Program. A dream romance is blossoming until Peter airs his views on girls and their careers. Instantly the summer turns sour. Will Peter ever admit he's wrong?

☐ **#53 GHOST OF A CHANCE by Janet Quin-Harkin On sale December 15, 1983 • 23939-2 • $1.95)**
—Meredith's not happy about spending the summer taking care of her sick aunt in Maine. The weather is miserable, she's stuck inside a spooky old beach house, and worst of all, her boyfriend Peter is a thousand miles away. Meredith resigns herself to daydreaming—until she meets Nat Franklin. Will she be able to stay true to Peter during her summer by the sea?

□ **#54 I CAN'T FORGET YOU by Lois I. Fisher (On sale December 15, 1983 • 23940-6 • $1.95)**
—When Jeri and Kemp went out together last year, they were always going to movies, parties, dances—it was wonderful. But when her grades began to slide, Jeri had to choose her schoolwork over Kemp. For a while, she was sure she'd done the right thing. Her grades went up, and then she met serious, sensitive Ben, and they shared a lot of quiet good times. But she can't forgt Kemp—and it seems that he feels just the same.

Buy these books at your local bookstore or use this handy coupon for ordering:

within her grasp. It doesn't matter that Enid is Elizabeth's best friend—or that revealing the secret may cost Enid both her reputation and the boy she loves.

☐ #3 PLAYING WITH FIRE (On sale November 15, 1983 • 23972-4 • $2.25)

Elizabeth doesn't trust Jessica's new boyfriend, Bruce Patman, one bit. He's arrogant, demanding—and way too fast. Jessica follows him everywhere, drops everything just to spend time with him. Jessica can usually hold her own with any guy, but this time Elizabeth's afraid Jessica may be going too far. . . .

☐ #4 POWER PLAY (On sale December 15, 1983 • 23730-6 • $2.25)

Small, round Robin Wilson follows golden girl Jessica Wakefield around like a puppy. Jessica is everything that Robin isn't: beautiful, popular, and president of Pi Beta Alpha, the most exclusive and chic sorority at Sweet Valley High. Robin has her heart set on pledging—and to Jessica's complete astonishment, her own sister is determined to help!

Buy these books at your local bookstore or use this handy coupon for ordering: